BABY CHASE

BABY CHASE

BY

HANNAH BERNARD

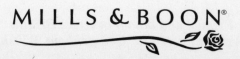

MILLS & BOON®

To Pam.
You'd better know why! :-)

First published in Great Britain 2003
Large Print edition 2003
Harlequin Mills & Boon Limited,
Eton House, 18-24 Paradise Road,
Richmond, Surrey TW9 1SR

© Hannah Bernard 2003

ISBN 0 263 17938 9

Set in Times Roman 16½ on 17½ pt.
16-0903-58798

Printed and bound in Great Britain
by Antony Rowe Ltd, Chippenham, Wiltshire

CHAPTER ONE

OF COURSE.

As soon as the legs appeared at the edge of the bed and the bedsprings creaked under the intruder's weight, Erin realized who he was. She let out a silent breath as the terrified pounding of her heart slowed. Of course there was no burglar in the house; no psychotic killer or rapist. It was Nathan Chase.

The intense relief was quickly followed by embarrassed dismay. The fabled Nathan was here, sitting on the bed in the guest room. And here she was, lying under that bed, clad only in a towel, with another one wrapped around her wet hair.

Erin stifled a sigh, cursing her own stupidity. Her sister-in-law had told her in a hasty last-minute message that her brother would arrive this week and stay overnight. Sally had assured her that she would not even notice him—if true to form, he would arrive around midnight and be gone early the next morning. Erin had hoped that would be true; she had no interest in meeting Sally's insensitive clod of a brother who didn't seem to give a damn about his own family.

Nevertheless, she should have been expecting him, instead of panicking when hearing noises downstairs after coming out of the shower. After briefly cursing her brother—it just had to be the one time she was house-sitting that his house was broken into—she had run into the empty guest room and crawled under the bed. Her instincts told her that the burglar would quickly pass the unused, almost empty room, allowing her to crawl from under the bed and escape to the roof through the window.

But there was no burglar. It was only Sally's brother, stopping for the night before he flew to the next corner of the world suffering war, famine or pestilence.

He still hadn't moved. Erin stared at his legs: black jeans and black socks. With… She narrowed her eyes. Did the man really have two smiling bunny rabbits on his socks?

She rolled her eyes when she noticed exactly what those bunny rabbits were doing. How typically juvenile. Her first impressions confirmed her long-established opinion of

Nathan Chase, even if first impressions were only of the man's socks. It was time to end this farce, say hello and goodbye to the man and escape.

Still she hesitated. The room was silent. She could hardly make out Nathan's breathing. What was the best way to alert him to her presence? A polite "Excuse me" from under the bed? A tap on his calf?

Crawling from under the bed, wearing nothing but two skimpy towels and a blanket of dust, would scare the man half to death. Even with her poor opinion of Sally's brother, she did not want to give him a heart attack. It might not make a great first impression.

He would take a shower, she suddenly realized. After all, he had just flown halfway across the world. At the very least he would go to the bathroom. That would give her ample time to escape the room. She smiled in relief at this easy solution and settled down for the wait, trying to get comfortable on the wooden floor without making a noise. It wasn't long until Nathan gave a deep sigh and stood up.

With a triumphant smile, Erin was on her side, ready to make her escape, when the jeans were suddenly whisked away and thrown over the foot of the bed. A second later the rabbits had also said their goodbyes. Before she got more than a glimpse of the muscular calves, the door was shut and the light went out. The bedsprings sagged dangerously close and peppered her face with dust.

Erin almost groaned aloud. Nathan was not co-operating. It was just like Sally's superman brother not to succumb to normal human needs like using the bathroom. She'd have to crawl out, scare the heck out of him and look like a complete idiot in the process. Gone was the opportunity to explain her mistake and escape with some dignity.

Or was it? How long did it take a person to fall asleep? Someone exhausted and jet-lagged? Surely he would be dead to the world in a few minutes. She would wait a while, then tiptoe out of the room—he'd never know she'd been there.

Carefully she stretched her cramped muscles, settling in for a longer wait. This will be a piece of cake, she told herself sternly. All she had to do was ignore the hard floor for a few minutes, and she would be home safe.

Just a few minutes.

Involuntarily, she shivered, goose bumps running up and down her body. A breeze from the window licked her skin with a frigid tongue. She struggled to convince herself it wasn't that cold, but her body refused to be convinced, pointing out that two damp towels were not helping the situation.

Determined to take her mind off the numerous sources of discomfort, she concentrated on Nathan's breathing. How much time had passed since her frantic dive under the bed? Was he asleep yet? His breathing was even and regular now, but was it the breathing of a man asleep?

Frustrated, she admitted she couldn't tell. Not used to sharing a bed with a man, she had no clue on how to interpret the breath patterns of this particular specimen. Was this fast-asleep breathing or just-about-to-fall-asleep breathing, or even can't-fall-asleep breathing?

The mattress had not moved since he'd lain down. Maybe he snored, she thought, heart lifting a fraction. That would give her a sure indication that he was out.

After forcing herself to count two hundred of his breaths, Erin decided he'd fallen asleep

and he did not snore. She refused to even con-
template the idea that he was still awake.

One inch at a time, she pushed herself out
from beneath the bed, taking care to bring the
towels with her. From her prone position she
saw the narrow frame of light from the hall,
but nevertheless the door was firmly shut.

Darn! She had forgotten that door.

Knowing this house as she did, she knew
that unless Nathan Chase was an exceptionally
heavy sleeper she didn't stand a chance of
opening that squeaky door without waking
him.

Turning her head to look up at the sleeping
man, she could barely make out his head,
turned away on the pillow, and the shape of
his body under the covers. He was fast asleep.
What a relief.

The cold breeze reminded her of the open
window. Of course! That escape route was the
reason she'd ended up in this mess in the first
place. From the roof she would be able to
climb back in through her own window.

She rose slowly, freezing when she realized
that the light from the full moon on the sleeping man's face had now been replaced by her
shadow. He moved restlessly, turning his face

towards her. Erin stood transfixed. She dared
not move, fearing he would awaken should the
moonlight again touch his face.

Finally, murmuring incomprehensibly, he
rolled over on his stomach, turning a broad
back to her. Erin relaxed slightly. She would
make it after all. In one swift movement she
was at the window. She clambered out onto
the roof, then paused for a moment to listen
for sounds from inside. There were none and
she managed to close the window without a
single creak.

November in Maine was not the time or
place to be prancing around on rooftops wearing a towel, but she'd ignore that for the moment. She was free. With a victorious smile
she started towards her own window.

She didn't get very far. The towel had
caught in the closed window. She tugged on
it, then was suddenly released as the window
opened. With a small shriek, Erin fell on her
side and started to slide down the slanting roof,
feet first.

A hand shot out and grabbed her arm.

Erin rested her forehead on the cold roof and
groaned. This couldn't be happening. This
kind of thing simply did not happen to her. She

was lying face down, the towel bunched up under her armpits. The man holding on to her arm was definitely getting a good view of her rear from the waist down.

It was almost preferable to looking him in the face.

Almost.

Erin grabbed on to the window ledge and pulled herself up on her knees, yanking her wrist from his grasp. She quickly tugged the towel back into position and, bracing herself, looked at the man standing inside, his arms crossed on his chest as he stared perplexed at her.

Nathan Chase, hot-shot news photographer, heartless brother of her beloved sister-in-law.

She'd never met him before, but Sally proudly displayed a picture of her brother in their living room, an enlarged but somewhat blurry snapshot of the two of them white-water rafting. It was too dark for her to see if he'd changed much in the ten years since that picture was taken. All she could see was a silhouette of his torso and sleep-tousled hair hanging down over the faint glint of his eyes.

She took a deep breath of the cool night air before speaking.

"Um. Hi. Hello. Good evening." She extended her hand. "You must be Nathan. I'm Erin, Thomas's sister; you've probably heard of me?"

Nathan's suspicious look at her outstretched hand was hilarious and the absurdity of the situation finally got the better of her. Biting her lip, she tried to get a hold of herself, but failed. She collapsed in a fit of giggles.

"Maybe...maybe I could come in?" she managed between fits of mirth, realizing that her giggles were not helping her regain her dignity. But she couldn't stop laughing.

He must think she was quite insane.

Nathan wondered for a moment if his sleep-deprived mind was playing tricks on him. He had fallen asleep the moment he'd hit the bed, but noises at the window managed to rouse him what seemed like only minutes later. He had expected to find a tree branch or even a bird pecking at the window, not a dusty temptress clad in goose-bumps, moonshine and a nervous grin.

And a towel. There was a towel too.

Cold wind brushed over his bare skin, reminding him that the woman must be freezing.

He moved away from the window, holding out a hand to help her in. Her small hand was icy in his palm as she climbed through the window, still giggling as she landed on her feet in front of him. Almost on reflex, he kept her cold hand between his and gently rubbed heat into it.

"You're Thomas's sister, Erin?" he repeated at last, finding his voice hoarse from sleep and exhaustion. He frowned as he struggled to remember what little he knew about Thomas's family and the sister he had known would be staying here. "The...librarian?"

He stared at her with amazement as he continued to rub heat into her hand. Admittedly, it had been quite a while since his last visit to a library, but this woman did not fit his image of a librarian, neither in looks nor behavior.

"My horn-rimmed glasses are in my room, and the bun came loose in the shower," she said solemnly before pulling her hands from his grasp. "I apologize for my unprofessional appearance."

OK, obviously she had come across librarian stereotypes before.

She backed towards the door and, to his regret, out of the moonlight that painted such a delicious pattern of colors over her skin. "Sally has told me so much about her big brother," she chattered. "It's nice to finally meet you."

"I definitely should have paid more attention when she talked about you," he murmured. "Just what were you doing out there, Miss Librarian? I know my brother-in-law is an innovative man around the house, but even he would draw the line at installing a hot tub up on the roof."

"Well…" she gestured vaguely "…I thought you were a burglar. It's a long story. Perhaps we'd better catch up on it later. I'm sure you need a good night's sleep after your journey." She began to move towards the door, but Nathan was finally fully awake and wasn't about to let her off the hook so easily. Not now that he was just beginning to enjoy himself.

"Not so fast." He stopped her with a hand on her shoulder, turning her around. Her shoulders were icy too, and he promised himself he would let her go in a minute so she could get warm. This was just too much fun to miss.

Telling himself he was simply making up for keeping her out of her bed, he kept his hand on her shoulder, feeling the heat radiate to her cold skin. The contact roused almost forgotten sensations inside him. It had been a long time since he had touched a woman. For that matter, it had been ages since he had even touched another human being.

For too long, his role had been simply that of an observer.

He pushed the thought aside and allowed his usual sense of humor to resurface and drown the heavy musings. He let go of her and crossed his arms on his chest again.

"I think you owe me a decent explanation," he said firmly, grinning inside. "How do I even know you're really Thomas's sister? You could be anyone."

To his delight she took him at his word and gasped in affronted outrage, her sense of humor about the situation obviously dissipated. "You think I'm a burglar? Why...! Does this look like a burglar's outfit?" she burst out, waving a hand at her grimy towel.

Nathan bit back a grin, and took a step back. He pretended to examine her attire thoughtfully, watching her face with amusement as she realized with a shock that she was not the most undressed person in the room.

"For heaven's sake, haven't you ever heard of pyjamas?" she asked, exasperated, aiming her gaze high on the wall behind his head. With a quick, angry movement she pulled the towel from her head, releasing a flow of damp curls onto her bare shoulders, and thrust it at him, eyes still averted.

Even in the faint light, Nathan could swear she was blushing. How intriguing. How...librarianish. With an amused chuckle he accepted the towel and tied it loosely around his waist. "I didn't expect to be rescuing nude damsels stuck on rooftops tonight," he replied. "If I'd known I assure you I would have dressed for the occasion." He grinned. "A red cape and tights come to mind."

Her eyes moved to the door again as she inched closer to the escape route. She started shivering theatrically to emphasize her state.

Nathan promised himself he would let her off the hook in just a minute. She needed to get warm, but after all, he could think of better ways to warm up a woman than to send her off alone to the shower. It wouldn't hurt to run those possibilities by her. Just as food for thought, of course.

He moved closer, trapping her between the door and his body without touching her. "You're going to leave just like that?"

His red-haired librarian seemed speechless. She was staring up at him like a doe caught in headlights, but her expression was one of surprise and suspicion, not of fear. It could be a trick of the moonlight, but he even thought he detected a flicker of awareness in those large eyes.

This had definite potential.

Nathan disregarded the little voice telling him to stop teasing her. His life had been savage lately, but he was still too much a gentleman to seduce his sister's friend in this situation. But she intrigued him, and for some reason he felt himself craving a taste of her. He wanted to feel those red curls against his face, wanted to entangle his fingers in them as he kissed her senseless and pulled that towel away...

It's been too long. OK, but don't take it out on a librarian!

Ignoring the stern voice of his own conscience, Nathan let his hands rest on the door on each side of her head, forming a tiny prison for his prey. He shook his head and tsked.

"I've never let a babe leave my bedroom without a goodbye kiss."

"What?" she croaked. "A *babe?*"

"A goodbye kiss," he repeated. "How about it?"

Erin swallowed nervously, clutching her towel with a death grip as she leaned back against the door. The glint in his eyes told her he was teasing her, and she was pretty sure she should be furious at his audacity. Something was stopping her fury from erupting though. Although he still wasn't touching her, he was close enough for his body heat to reach out and warm her. That was why she felt this pull towards him, she told herself, ignoring the insistent little voice that pointed out that she didn't really feel all that cold any more. Simple survival instincts. Being cold, she would naturally gravitate towards heat.

It certainly did not mean that she would let him kiss her, even when he made the offer in that low, sexy voice. It was bad enough that she was actually tempted to take him up on it. And for one thing, nobody had ever accused her of being a babe before.

The whole situation was surreal. For once she was grateful for Nathan's absence from his sister's life. She would never live this down.

"I don't think so, Mr Chase. I'm not one of those 'babes', and I'd appreciate it if you stopped blocking the door and let me get back to my own room. It's very late and I'm cold and tired."

"Call me Nathan," he said smoothly, ignoring her outburst. "After all, you're standing naked in my bedroom. Plus, you claim you're family."

That did it. At last her long-repressed anger at the absent Nathan Chase came to the fore. She took a deep breath, and then the words erupted. "I am family, you inconsiderate bastard!" she hissed. "If you'd cared enough to come to your sister's wedding or to the baby's christening or to any of the Christmas gatherings, or even a single family barbecue, you'd know who I am."

She had been venting her anger at him for years in her mind. It all came pouring out now. "Do you know that your sister almost canceled her first holiday in three years, just because you'd be staying here for, what, all of six hours? It took all of mine and Thomas's persuasive skills to convince her to go.'' She jabbed her finger into his chest. ''And your father's funeral? No, you were too busy taking snapshots and picking up *babes* on the other side of the world. And your sister's wedding? She so wanted you to give her away. Until the last minute she hoped you'd suddenly show up. When you didn't she walked alone down the aisle and spent half the reception making excuses for you!'' She stopped for a breath. ''Half her friends think you're a myth! You didn't even attend the baby's christening. Your sister named her daughter after you, but you couldn't even spare a few hours to visit! She's almost a year old and you've never even seen her! And then you dare show up here, wearing a pair of perverted rabbits, and of course you pick a time when they aren't even here!''

Nathan was standing still in front of her, body tense, his features stony. Erin closed her mouth, then her eyes. There was silence for a long moment, but she kept her eyes closed, hoping the scene would just vanish and she'd wake up sweating in her bed. This had to be a nightmare.

At last he spoke.

''Perverted rabbits?''

She let out a heavy breath. Obviously, and perhaps *unfortunately*, her speech hadn't hurt his feelings. His voice reflected no emotion other than amusement. Nothing she had said meant anything to him. Of course not. If the man had feelings, he wouldn't behave the way he did towards his own family.

But she had no right to betray Sally's feelings like that. Her sister-in-law never complained about her brother's behavior or questioned the validity of his excuses.

She felt something touch her shoulders and realized he had draped his shirt over them. Defeated, she accepted the gesture, and put her arms one at a time in the sleeves, but gave up trying to fasten the buttons while still holding the towel in place.

''Are we discussing the moral message of my socks now?''

The humor in his voice tugged at her mouth, threatening to pull up its corners. She resisted. He would not charm his way around her even if he did everyone else.

''Actually, Erin, you know nothing about me, or my rabbits. And, you know, I believe those creatures are engaging in perfectly normal conduct for the rabbit species.'' He began buttoning the shirt for her, without, she conceded, even so much as brushing a finger against her body.

"Nothing perverted about them. There," he added, fastening the last button. "You're decent now, Librarian."

"Right." She couldn't believe she had allowed him to dress her like a child. This night had to be the weirdest one of her life. Shaking her head in disbelief, she turned the doorknob. Once again, he stopped her, this time with his fingers circling her wrist.

"You were in my room before I went to sleep, weren't you? You saw my socks when I was getting undressed."

She nodded.

"Did you enjoy the show?"

"I was hiding under the bed," she snapped. "I didn't see anything except those darn socks!"

"Too bad," he muttered, "I'll have to give you a repeat performance some time." He released her wrist, only to put a finger to her cheek and turn her head so their eyes met. His smile was wicked. "Next time I strip for you, I'll put more feeling into it."

Once again, Erin opened her mouth, only to close it again, firmly banishing the tempting mental images to the basement of her mind. He reached towards her again and she jumped. Raising an eyebrow, Nathan reached past her to the door and pulled it open.

"Goodnight, Miss Librarian," he murmured. "It's been a pleasure. I'll take a rain check on that kiss."

Erin's anger surged again as she escaped from his room. His door shut quietly behind her a second before she slammed her own door shut and collapsed on the bed.

What a bastard! She slapped her pillow a few times, then grabbed her hairbrush and brushed her hair into shape with quick, angry movements. What an unfeeling bastard! He didn't care how he hurt his little sister. And grinning all the time, as if this was all one big joke. She threw the hairbrush on the nightstand, the towel across a chair, and crawled into bed. Grateful for its warmth and softness, she pulled the covers up to her chin.

As her anger slowly subsided, that insistent voice in her head reclaimed center stage. Never before had she experienced such an instant attraction to a man. And that to someone she had disliked from afar for years. She groaned, and pulled the covers over her head as she began to wonder what would have happened if she had agreed to that kiss. The kiss that might have happened, she admitted, if he hadn't roused her fury with that conceited crack about babes.

With a sinking feeling, she refused to let herself wonder. They had not kissed. They never would. Nathan Chase would be gone in the morning, and good riddance.

She turned on her side and punched her pillow into submission, then closed her eyes, determined to put the whole ridiculous episode behind her. He would be gone by the time she woke up and who knew when she would see him again? With any luck she would wake up thinking he was just a dream.

A bad dream.

CHAPTER TWO

Coffee.

Erin's nose twitched as she trudged barefoot and yawning out of her room. She smelled coffee. Yes, this *was* the smell of coffee, a drug she could absolutely use right now. She rubbed her eyes with the backs of her hands. The night had been filled with fragmented dreams as she'd hovered in the twilight zone between sleep and insomnia.

Coffee. The seductive aroma was irresistible. Her nose leading the way, she padded down the stairs.

It wasn't until she was almost at the bottom of the stairs that she realized the smell of coffee indicated the presence of another person in the house. That other person could only be Nathan. She glanced at her wrist, then slapped the banister in annoyance. Her watch must still be in the bathroom where she had left it before taking that shower last night. A late sleeper, she considered it sacrilege to rise earlier than nine on a Sunday morning, and, considering how late she'd gone to bed last night, it must be close to noon now.

Nathan should be long gone, not sitting in the kitchen drinking the Colombian nectar of the gods.

For a moment she considered going back upstairs to get dressed, but rejected the idea. After all, she was the one house-sitting; he was the overnight guest. And it was not as if her practical cotton nightgowns came close to being seductive.

Coffee.

First coffee, then think.

The morning sun streamed in through the large kitchen window, reflecting off the spotless countertops. She stopped short and stared in disbelief. Spotless they had not been the previous evening. Who had done the dishes? Three days' worth of dishes? She squinted against the light and looked around. Nathan was sitting in the corner seat, *her* seat, she thought in annoyance—reading the morning paper, *her* paper, over a cup of coffee. *His* coffee, she acknowledged reluctantly.

''Morning,'' she mumbled in response to his cheerful greeting and quickly fetched orange juice from the fridge and popped bread in the toaster. She helped herself to a cup of the coffee and gulped half of it down while she made her breakfast and sat down at the table opposite Nathan.

The caffeine didn't take long to kick in, and as the fog in her mind began to lift she noticed from the corner of her eye that he had put his paper away and was scrutinizing her.

She still hadn't looked directly at his face. Last night the room had been lit only by moonlight, his face cast in shadows. She knew the shape of his features, the glint of eyes and teeth, the waves of hair, and the silhouette of his body, but she found herself reluctant to look at him in the light of day, to complete the picture.

"I wondered this morning if you had been a dream," Nathan murmured, laughter edging his voice. "It was you last night, wasn't it? On the roof? Wearing a skimpy blue towel?"

"The towel was yellow!" she corrected, stung for some reason. So much for an unforgettable experience.

He laughed. "You're right. The other towel was blue. The one you so graciously gave to me." He looked her up and down. "Anyway, my shirt becomes you even better than the towel did.''

Erin blinked and looked down at herself. She wasn't wearing one of her nightgowns after all; she was still wearing Nathan's shirt, the one he had dressed her in last night.

Heat flushed her cheeks. Her hands went to the buttons of the shirt, as if to return it right away, but her brain managed to stop them in time.

''I'm sorry, I didn't realize I still had that on,'' she muttered. ''You'll get it back today.''

''No hurry. We really got off on the wrong foot last night. Maybe we should start over.''

She made a noncommittal sound.

''You haven't looked at me once. Did I frighten you last night? I'm sorry if I did.''

Lifting her head, she forced herself to look at his face. Clinically, she ticked his features off one by one. Black hair with the faintest red highlights where the morning sun grazed it. Too long, for her conservative taste, curling towards his collar at the back. Strong chin and cheekbones, firm mouth, curved in what seemed to be a permanent half-smile. Laughter lines around his mouth and eyes. Gritting her teeth, she allowed their gazes to meet. Green eyes. Deep, vibrant green.

The man looked even better than his pictures.

Better than the teasing shadow that had haunted her dreams last night.

No wonder that her dreams had revolved around him, she thought, glancing at the soft fabric of his shirt over her breasts. There was something intensely intimate about wearing a man's shirt to bed.

Mentally she shook herself. Nathan had asked her a question several minutes ago. He might expect an answer.

''You didn't frighten me,'' she told him. ''Of course I was scared at first, when I thought someone had broken into the house, but the rest was just embarrassing. I'd just like to forget all about it.''

What was embarrassing was her knowledge of that instant response to him, that pull of attraction towards a man she didn't know but already disliked.

Nathan chuckled. ''It was funny. As I recall, you found it funny too at the time. You almost fell off the roof laughing.'' He extended a hand towards her. "Let's start over. Hello, Erin. I'm Nathan. Nice to meet you."

Charm on, full impulse, she thought sourly, looking into smiling green eyes filled with confidence and self-assurance. *Well, it's not going to work with me, buddy. I'm not one of your babes. I won't succumb to that charm of yours again.*

Reluctantly she shook his hand, feeling its warmth shoot up her arm with the speed of light. Irritated, she concentrated on her breakfast, answering his few attempts at conversation with one-syllable words. There was no reason to engage in small talk with him. Perhaps she was being rude, but better that than to embarrass herself again.

She put her cup down after finishing the last dregs of coffee and glanced up at the kitchen clock. It was almost eleven. Nathan had stayed almost double the allotted six hours. He would probably leave right after breakfast.

Perhaps she could manage to be civil just for another hour. For Sally's sake.

Determined to do her best, she straightened up from her slouch and offered him more coffee. With a slight look of surprise, he accepted.

"Sally said you wouldn't be staying long."

Nathan took a sip of his coffee, then ran a hand through his hair. "Actually, I will be staying a while."

"Oh," she muttered. There must have been a change of plan. She might have to put up with him a bit longer. Without thinking, she sighed.

Nathan raised an eyebrow, the half-smile turning sardonic. "No need to sound as if your world is collapsing. There is room enough in this house for the two of us."

"Are there no hot opportunities or *babes* awaiting you?"

He stared at her until she began squirming in her seat.

"You really dislike me, don't you?" he asked at last. Erin thought his voice reflected boredom more than anything else. She bit her tongue to hold back the angry words, but they fought their way out anyway.

"I love Sally. She is my friend and my brother's wife. I dislike it when people hurt her."

Something flickered in his eyes. It could have been guilt or remorse, but she was more inclined to interpret it as irritation or even amusement.

"Has my sister said that I hurt her?"

"She doesn't need to," she snapped back. "It is obvious in her face every time she hopes that you will deign to come home and you don't."

"I see."

"What kind of a man misses his own father's funeral, for God's sake?"

The outrage in her voice didn't seem to affect him in the least. He sipped his coffee calmly and did not flinch from her incensed gaze. "I don't know, Erin. What kind of a man does that and then comes home sporting perverted rabbits on his socks?"

Erin shook her head in disbelief. "Life is just one big joke to you, isn't it?"

"Absolutely. An attitude I can heartily recommend. It's the only way to keep your sanity in this world." He gave her a small smile. "You've made your point. I'm an unfeeling bastard. Fine. Can we now agree to a truce while we're sharing this house?"

"Just how long will you be staying, then?"

"A while."

"How long is a 'while'?"

"I'm not sure. I'll be here at least until after Christmas."

Erin's refilled cup almost didn't survive the trip to the table, spilling precious drops on the white surface.

"After Christmas?"

"Yep." He seemed unfazed by her obvious consternation, calmly mopping up the spilled coffee with a paper towel.

She groaned and hid her face in her hands. This was a disaster. She had been counting on having this time alone, to think things through and to make plans for the baby. She had taken time off this week, just for that purpose.

"I take it that's a problem for you?"

"Sally said you would only stay the night," she moaned. "If I'd known you were staying, I could have made other arrangements. I wouldn't have sublet my apartment."

The telephone on the wall rang and Erin answered it morosely, thinking that if he were a gentleman he would offer to move out and check into a hotel. After all, it was only a month until Thomas and Sally returned.

Right on cue, it was her sister-in-law, shouting through a tunnel of static, asking if her brother had arrived yet.

"I'm so glad you got to meet Nathan, Erin!" Enthusiasm all but bubbled out of the phone. "Isn't he terrific?"

"I'm sure he is," Erin replied diplomatically, and was rewarded by a prolonged long-distance monologue about Nathan's virtues.

"Is he there? Can I talk to him for a minute?"

"Of course, I'll get him. Give Thomas and Natalie a hug from me."

Nathan hardly got a word in edgeways during the short conversation with his sister. His attempts consisted of a few words that were interrupted every time.

She smiled into her coffee. So even Nathan Chase succumbed to the charm of Sally's bulldozer personality.

With a wry grin, Nathan handed her back the phone and her sister-in-law's excited voice was again echoing in her ear.

"Hi again, Erin. I told Nathan you would look after him for me, show him around and stuff."

Erin's mouth fell open as her accusing gaze flew to Nathan. He shrugged and shook his head, then picked up the paper again and started reading.

"What? I can't…"

"He's never stopped in town for longer than a few hours; he hasn't seen anything. Maybe you could also go to the theater or something. Anything you can think of."

"I'm not…"

"I really appreciate it, Erin. I'm just devastated not to be home for my brother, but I know you'll do everything you can for him…"

After a few moments of chatter, Sally hung up and Erin was left standing with her mouth open, holding the phone in one hand.

Nathan pretended to concentrate on his paper, while trying to control the grin fighting its way to his face. The other pawn in his sister's game obviously had no clue about the stakes. He felt Erin's stabbing gaze on the back of his head and it wasn't hard to picture the fury clouding her delicate features. Apart from her giggles last night, she seemed to have a permanent scowl etched on her brow. Did the woman ever smile?

"Don't worry, Erin," he said without looking up. "Sally never needs to know that you didn't play tour guide for me and I certainly don't expect you to."

"She'll know," Erin muttered, throwing herself back into her chair. "Sally always finds out things like that."

He shrugged. "Fine. I'll tell her I preferred to be on my own. She may even take the hint and not throw us together again."

Erin's head snapped up, brows drawn together. "Throw us together? What do you mean?"

He looked up, allowing the grin to surface. "What else?"

Her mouth hung open. "You mean she knew you would be staying longer and she deliberately didn't tell me?"

He shrugged. "I'm afraid my sister fancies herself as something of a matchmaker."

"Matchmaker?" With amusement he watched the emotions play across her face. "You mean she thought you and I...?" She sputtered. "What a ridiculous idea!"

Nathan nodded. "Couldn't agree more."

Knowing his reply had been less than flattering, he watched with amusement as relief flirted with bruised dignity in her expressive features.

"And you didn't object to being sent here to play house with a total stranger?"

He shrugged again. "Why should I? I've shared a bed with fleas and dogs, I can share a house with a librarian." He smiled faintly. "To tell you the truth, I thought you might make a nice change."

Her hands clenched into fists, Erin jumped to her feet, anger flashing from her eyes, the soft fabric of his shirt rising and falling with her deep, indignant breaths. "Oh, did you? A nice change from fleas and dogs? Or did you mean a nice change from your *babes?* Is this the let's-seduce-the-librarian week? I am not a toy, I'm not a *babe* and I'm absolutely not a 'nice change'!"

Nathan raised his hands in supplication. "I didn't mean it like that, Erin! I certainly had no seduction plans. And would you please stop mentioning the word babes in every other sentence?"

She waited, hands on hips. "In what way did you mean it, then?"

He shrugged. "I simply meant I'd enjoy having some female company without having to flirt or play games. I thought we might enjoy some civil, polite conversation over cereal or TV dinners. Perhaps even play Scrabble or

Trivial Pursuit.'' He grinned at her. ''You know, librarian stuff.''

''You don't know anything about librarians.''

''I'm beginning to realize that. No glasses perched on that nose.'' His gaze lifted to her hair. ''And no bun this morning either.''

''Sorry to disappoint you,'' she muttered.

Nathan's grin faded, leaving a lopsided smile. ''Whatever else you are, Miss Librarian, you are certainly not a disappointment.''

The doorbell, combined with insistent knocking, interrupted any explanation of that cryptic remark. As Erin opened the front door after a brief glance through the peephole, two miniature redheads fought for a place in her arms. ''Mom says you might take us swimming!'' a piping voice yelled as Erin looked out to see a waving arm as her mother's gray car sped away.

Inwardly she groaned, although she was careful not to let on to the twins that they were less than welcome. Her mother kept doing that. She loved her little brothers, and they stayed with her often, but Mom took blatant advantage of her protectiveness.

"Hey, guys!" She knelt down and hugged the five-year-olds. "How long do I get to keep you today?"

"Until tomorrow!" Samuel jumped up and down, trying to reach the coat-hanger. "Mom says that there's plenty of room because Tom and Sally are away."

Grinding her teeth, Erin forced a smile as she helped the boys hang up their jackets. She wouldn't have minded having them staying this weekend, especially with Nathan in the house, but she would have appreciated being asked.

"Hello!" Nathan appeared in the kitchen door and smiled at the boys, then looked at Erin. "I can see the resemblance. Are they yours?"

"Noooo," the twins said in unison. They were used to this question but it never failed to disgust them. "She's not our mother, she's our sister!" Daniel added.

The boys stared curiously at him.

"Are you Erin's boyfriend?" Daniel asked.

Nathan shook his head with a smile. "I'm afraid not."

"Oh." The child looked dejected. "Mom says we can't have little brothers, but if Erin finds a boyfriend and gets married then we can have little nephews instead.''

''You already have a little niece,'' Erin reminded her brothers. ''Soon she'll be old enough to play with you.''

''She's a girl!'' Samuel pointed out indignantly. ''Do you have any boys?'' he asked Nathan.

He shook his head. ''No little boys and no little girls.''

''How come?''

''Well...I don't have a wife, for one.''

''You should get one,'' Samuel advised, looking very serious. ''When girls become wives, then they are OK. You get to cuddle up to them in bed and everything.''

A corner of Nathan's mouth twitched. ''That is a bonus,'' he agreed solemnly. ''It can get lonely in bed.''

''Yes,'' Daniel chimed in. ''But if you don't have a wife, you can snuggle up to a teddy instead. Do you have a teddy bear?''

''Well...no.''

Daniel nodded, his little face serious. ''You should get a wife. They're better. Sometimes they also make brownies.''

"You little chauvinist…" Erin muttered under her breath, grinning as Nathan fought to hold back his laughter. Losing interest in marriage counseling, the boys scampered off, heading for the small office, to Thomas's computer.

"I didn't know Tom had little brothers."

"There is a lot you don't know about this family," Erin said, then bit her tongue. She would have to live with this man for a whole month. It wouldn't do to keep attacking him the whole time. Softening her voice, she continued, "We also have a little sister on our father's side. Her name is Alexandra and she is only three."

"I see. And you have a twin sister, don't you?"

She nodded. "Erika. She's a lawyer."

"Your parents must have been very young when they had the three of you."

She nodded, then followed the boys into the office. Nathan followed her in, and the two little chauvinists pounced directly on him as a fellow computer patriot.

"Would you sit with them just five minutes while I get dressed?" she asked Nathan, reluctant to ask him for a favour, but not wanting to leave the boys alone with all the expensive equipment. Thomas had spent a great deal of time teaching his brothers how to play with his computer without damaging anything, and they were fast learners, but she didn't quite trust them yet.

"Of course." He smiled at the boys. "I bet there is a game or two you can show me, isn't there?"

"Yeah!" the boys chorused with enthusiasm. "There is this one with demons and dragons where you have a sledgehammer..." One twin shushed the other and both glanced at Erin.

She couldn't help but laugh. "Nathan, just use your best judgment. Nothing too bloody."

Smiling, Nathan lifted one boy up and sat down at the computer, holding him in his lap. "We'll be fine. Don't hurry on our account."

Erin ran upstairs to her room. She replaced Nathan's shirt with jeans and a white sweater, and brushed her hair. Her brothers had interrupted just in time, or she would probably have attacked Nathan again. And she shouldn't: after all, what he did or did not do was none of her business. Somehow that man managed to push all her buttons. She wasn't a confronta-

tional type; in fact she had the opposite problem of avoiding conflict rather than facing it.
Her temper had never matched the color of her
hair, and she had always done her best to get
along with people.

Nathan Chase was not going to change that.
She was going to be polite and nice to him.
He was family after all. He was right—it was
none of her business how he spent his time.
And it was not his fault that Sally had decided
to make them live together. She could even
forgive him for that conceited teasing last
night. After all, the circumstances were bizarre
and the man half-asleep.

She grabbed the shirt and headed for the
washing machine, stuffing it inside before she
succumbed to the temptation of holding it to
her face and inhaling his scent. That shirt had
already got her in enough trouble in dream-
land. She paused, a bottle of detergent in her
hand, reflecting on her feelings and not liking
them one bit. She responded strongly to his
presence, there was no denying that. Perhaps
her anger worked to mask her attraction to
him.

No.

She shook her head firmly and finished her chore. She did not want a man in her life at all, especially now. Even if she did, she reminded herself, he had made it clear he considered Sally's matchmaking idea ridiculous. She ignored the small sting this thought cost. It was for the best. She would be friendly to Nathan, because he meant so much to Sally, she would stay out of his way, and soon all this would be over.

Soon she would have her baby.

The three males were engrossed in a flying simulator when she came back downstairs. Nathan looked briefly up and acknowledged her with a small smile, but did not seem to be in a hurry to get away. Quietly she sat down in the easy chair in the corner, watching them. The picture of Nathan playing with her two little brothers clashed with her mental image of the cold and aloof man who didn't care enough to see his own niece.

"Tom is our big brother. He is a programmer," Samuel boasted to Nathan while his brother had control of the joystick. "He tells the computers what to do. Can you do that?"

"Not as well as Tom, no. I'm a photographer. I take pictures."

"You take pictures?" Daniel flew his plane over enemy territory, bombarding a fleet of ships below. He did not sound too impressed. "Just ordinary pictures?"

Nathan chuckled. "Yes. Just ordinary pictures."

Erin thought back to Sally's scrapbooks, holding hundreds of clippings, all Nathan's pictures from every corner of the globe. None of them could be called ordinary. Even in her own biased judgment, the quality of his work was indisputable. His photos were stark and unflinching, pulling the viewer in and not letting go until a point had been made.

"Can you do magic?"

She watched Nathan frown as he tried to follow the child's train of thought. "Magic?"

"Mom took us to a photographer once. He did magic tricks. Mom said he did that to make us laugh."

"I'm not that kind of a photographer."

"What kind, then?"

"I take pictures for the newspapers," Nathan explained. "Do you guys have a camera?"

The twins shook their heads.

He stood up and deposited one little boy back on the chair. "I'll show you mine," he said, returning a few minutes later with his camera bag. The boys abandoned the computer game and crowded around him as he opened it and showed them the different lenses and tools, even allowing them to handle the delicate equipment.

"Be careful!" she reminded the boys. "Nathan, they're only kids. Don't let them damage anything."

To her amazement, the two hyperactive youngsters sat quietly and listened as Nathan explained in simple terms how the camera worked and how to take good pictures. Then he got two disposable cameras from his pack and gave one to each boy. "They're even waterproof," he told them with a smile. "If you're going swimming with your sister, you can take pictures underwater."

"Wow!" the boys echoed in unison. Erin grinned. Both boys loved the swimming pool, and she often took them there, but both balked at putting their heads underwater. She had a feeling that was about to change.

"I'm going to take one of Your Boyfriend," Daniel yelled, running out of the room, followed by his brother. Their noisy footsteps echoed around the house as they trampled up the stairs.

"Your boyfriend? Your boyfriend is upstairs?" Nathan looked confused.

Erin chuckled. "Follow them and you'll see."

Looking quizzically at her, Nathan strode upstairs, following the sound of the twins' voices to her bedroom. She followed the crowd, finding the two boys up to their elbows in her fish tank, both pointing a camera at one of the two multicolored fishes swimming amidst swaying strands of greenery.

"Meet Your Boyfriend," Erin said, pointing at the male fish with the huge, colorful tail. "And next to him, Your Girlfriend."

"Interesting names."

"It's a long story. Originally they were called Romeo and Juliet. Then my sister began using Boyfriend and Girlfriend. That stuck, and the boys added the 'Your' to it. Don't ask me why."

"Are they Sally's?"

The room had never seemed small to her, but it seemed to have shrunk with his presence. No matter where she was standing, he was too close for comfort. She moved back, attempting to put some distance between them, and finally opted for sitting on the bed.

''No, they're mine. I couldn't very well leave them at my flat. They're my pets. But believe me, moving them was quite a challenge.''

Nathan leaned back, his elbows on the high window sill. He looked at her speculatively. ''I'd have taken you as more of a cat person.''

''I am,'' she confessed, ''but I'm allergic to most animals, especially cats and dogs. If I indulge myself and scratch a feline for a second my face puffs up and I cry non-stop for the next hour.'' She made a face. ''I'd have thought conditioning kicked in and relieved you of the longing to cuddle a kitten when you have to suffer as a consequence.''

Nathan chuckled. ''Allergies can be a pest.''

''Yes,'' she agreed in a heartfelt tone. ''Fortunately dust doesn't bother me, for some reason. If it did I'd have a hard time working in a library.'' She grinned sheepishly. ''And I would have sneezed under your bed and given you the fright of your life.''

Nathan's eyes sparkled with amusement. ''That would have been terrible. We'd have missed all the fun!''

Erin looked away and opened her arms as one little boy maneuvered himself into her lap. ''What were you doing under Uncle Nathan's bed?'' he demanded.

He was *Uncle* Nathan now? Some serious male bonding must have occurred while she had been getting dressed. Before she could come up with an explanation that would not reach her mother's ears, Nathan came to her rescue.

''We were playing hide and seek,'' he explained smoothly. Erin sent him a grateful look, but it went unnoticed as Nathan picked up a picture from the dresser.

''Is this Natalie?'' he asked.

He didn't even recognize the child.

Her softening attitude towards him hardened again and her voice was icy when she confirmed that the picture was of their niece. The changed tone of voice did not go unnoticed. He looked back at her, holding her gaze for

several seconds. Then he shrugged and replaced the picture, smiling again.

"Well, I need to be going." He glanced at
his watch, then pushed himself from the window and ruffled each boy's hair. "It was nice
meeting you guys. Perhaps I'll see you tonight.
You too, Librarian," he added with a grin,
reaching out to tousle her hair too. She yanked
her head back, and justice was served as he
snatched his hand away at the sting of static
electricity.

"Why don't you make him your boyfriend?" Samuel asked, thankfully after
Nathan had left the room.

"She can't, stupid; people who are related
can't be boyfriend and girlfriend."

"Nathan and I aren't related," she told the
boys.

"Yes, you are." Daniel looked very sure of
himself. "See, Nathan is related to Natalie and
Natalie is related to you, so he is related to
you."

"But Mom's related to us and we're related
to Daddy and they're married!" Samuel coun-
tered.

Erin grinned, pushing thoughts of Nathan and his family away. Logic lessons. Her favorite activity with the two growing minds.

Already it was dark outside. Nathan stretched out on the sofa and stared up at the ceiling. He could hear the faint sounds of Erin and the boys upstairs as she got them ready for bed. The unfamiliar sounds of children's voices and running water as the boys brushed their teeth reminded him of his own distant childhood. He frowned, dark brows coming together in a brooding line as old memories began eating at the barricades he had erected around himself for so long. He squeezed his eyes shut and shook his head. There was no use in thinking back, no purpose in reliving things no one could change.

This was why he hadn't been home in so long. Just being in his sister's house brought back memories he had decided long ago were best left untouched. He'd believed they had lost the power to hurt him, but he'd been wrong. To look on the bright side, he thought wryly, at least the nightmares he'd been suffering hadn't visited him last night. He might not like the fact that self-pitying thoughts about his childhood had erased the horrors he had witnessed on the job, but at least he had been able to sleep again.

With determination he forced his thoughts in another direction. By degrees, a smile began to warm his thoughts as they strayed to his reluctant housemate. She did think he was a complete bastard, he acknowledged with some regret, picturing the frost in her eyes when he had asked if the child in the picture was their niece. And she was probably right. He could have been more considerate of his sister's needs, even if he did not share her desire for contact. Although he had had parents and a sister, he had never really been a part of the family. He had told himself that staying away was for the best, not only for him but also for his parents and his sister. His family had never fully known the dangers he faced and he had been happy to have that excuse not to allow them participation in his life. Even after their parents' death, he had continued to convince himself that the lack of contact protected his sister from unnecessary worry. But perhaps he had inflicted hurt in its place.

Mentally he shrugged, pushing the regrets away. What's done is done.

His eyes closed, he forced his thoughts again to more pleasant matters. His mouth curved into a grin as he pictured the delectable curve of bottom and thigh on the roof. The smile widened as his mind's eye continued to replay the events of the previous night. The movement of her hair as she ripped the towel off her head and wordlessly ordered him to cover himself. The roundness of her breasts visible above her other towel.

He was deep into some very vivid illicit fantasies when a voice intruded.

''Nathan? Are you OK?''

Eyes flying open, he jumped guiltily to his feet. He shoved both hands through his hair and then carefully sat down again. Inwardly, he laughed at himself. Sure, he had been caught in a compromising situation before, but never alone.

She was standing in the doorway, looking at him with a frown of concern. ''Are you ill? Do you have a fever? You look hot.''

A series of possible responses ran through Nathan's mind, each one rejected by his stern super-ego.

Be nice, Nathan. She hasn't seen the nice side of you yet. You can be nice, can't you? You still remember how?

He cleared his throat. "I don't think so, no. I just…uh…fell asleep…"

She nodded. "The boys are asleep too. At last." She held up an oblong box. "I brought a peace offering."

Nathan gritted his teeth as he ordered his body to ignore the way her breasts moved under her sweater as she lifted her arm.

"Peace offering?" he managed to ask.

"Scrabble. Want to play?"

Nathan laughed. "You bet, Librarian." He winked. "Maybe you will make a nice change after all."

She looked at him suspiciously for a moment, but then smiled, to his relief accepting his humor at face value.

She was a worthy opponent, matching his every move. It did not help that in order to keep his promise to himself, Nathan had to reject all the best words that by themselves formed in his mind and on his slate. At the moment he could think of three words that would send her into a fit, with good reason. Regretfully he threw his last letters on the board to win the game with the innocent word LACES.

Of course, he would have preferred seeing her reaction to some of the other words, but he was trying really hard to be a gentleman here. For now.

As if she'd read his mind, her eyes met his and their gazes locked for a few tension-filled moments.

Erin felt herself tremble as their eyes met. His face was intense, dark pupils wide, firm lips slightly apart. His whole body was tense as unspoken messages flew between them. She could read them easily, with her intellect and her mind as well as with her heart. Non-verbal communication, body language, this was her field, what she had specialized in during those long years studying anthropology. She knew his heart must be picking up speed, his hormone system sending messages to different organs, his senses open to receive her every signal. In short: all the same things that were happening in her own treacherous body.

She could not be misreading him. The attraction was mutual and strong. How could she be feeling this for a man she didn't even like?

Throughout the day, he hadn't made it easy for her to keep disliking him, she admitted to herself. With his humor and constant smile, his easy way with her brothers, he kept charming her off her pedestal. She had to work at it, constantly remind herself of the thoughtless and cold way he treated his family.

She shook her head and clenched her eyes shut for one second, breaking the mood. Ignoring what they both knew, she smiled politely at him as she put the letters away.

"You're good. I'm not used to losing at Scrabble."

He held out his hand. "You're a very worthy opponent, Erin."

Erin took his hand and congratulated him. The warm pressure sent tingles up her arm until she pulled her hand away. But he had behaved. He hadn't even made one dubious word during the game, and heaven knew that plenty of them had somehow arranged themselves on her own slate.

She hesitated. "I'd like to apologize for my outburst last night and this morning. I had no right to criticize you like that. It really is none of my business."

Nathan folded the game and put it back into the box. "I was out of line too. I wasn't exactly a gentleman last night." He grinned at her. "I'm not used to finding half-naked librarians in my room at night. The devil in me took over."

Why did the devil in him have to be so darn appealing?

"OK, pardons are granted all around," she said breezily.

He held out his hand again. "Shall we shake on that?"

She hesitated a moment, then took his hand again, careful to slide her hand quickly out of his grasp again. Tingles once more. What was the man doing to her?

Nathan shifted his gaze from hers and out the window to the darkness beyond. "Actually, I've thought a lot about what you said," he said quietly. "I didn't realize Sally needed me. With the age difference we've never been close. She was only a child when I left home."

"Neither of you have any other blood relatives," Erin commented. "Apart from her daughter, you are her only living relative."

He shrugged, his posture turning defensive and his voice distant. "I do fine on my own.

Anyway, if I had known it meant so much to her, I would have tried to visit more often. I really didn't know. The fact is, I hardly know my sister. We're strangers to each other.''

Perhaps she had misjudged him. Perhaps not. She felt confused. He seemed contrite about having ignored his sister's needs, but he sounded very cold stating that he did fine on his own. How could he have failed to realize that his sister might need him after their father's sudden death?

"If you don't care, then why did you come back now?"

He glanced at her. "Are you getting personal again?"

His voice was friendly enough, but Erin recognized the warning for what it was.

"Anyway, you may not have been close," she said with hesitation, "but you are her older brother. Sisters tend to idolize older brothers."

Nathan chuckled, warm light appearing in his eyes, that in itself convincing her that he loved his sister deeply. "She used to follow me around like a puppy. She even hid in my car once, but I made sure she never did that again."

"You did?"

He frowned mockingly at her. "That's a chilling tone of voice, Erin. I didn't beat her. We had a serious discussion about privacy and safety, that's it. I'm not a monster."

"I never said you were. But…"

"Spit it out, Librarian."

Erin squirmed. "You were right. It's none of my business. But you've never even seen your little niece…" She let the question trail off.

"I look forward to seeing her," Nathan replied after a short but loaded silence.

Erin didn't push further. She stood up. "Well, I should be heading for bed. The boys will have me up at the crack of dawn. Goodnight."

"Goodnight." He smiled up at her, and she clenched her jaw as the sudden transformation of his face from serious to cheerful did wicked things to her insides. "See you tomorrow."

Tomorrow came all too soon. Predictably, the twins woke her up at seven. Yawning off the dreams she refused to acknowledge she remembered in detail, she got up, fed them as quietly as possible so they wouldn't disturb Nathan and was off to the indoor swimming pool by eight. As she had suspected, the lure of underwater pictures was enough to cure the twins of their fear of getting water in their faces.

The day passed quickly and they were home at four, just in time for their mother to arrive and pick the boys up.

"Thanks for having them," her mother said, shooing the twins out to her car.

The boys were out of earshot. "I would appreciate it next time if you'd ask me first, Mom. I could have had other plans."

"I don't think it's too much to ask that you watch your brothers once in a while," her mother snapped. "After all the sacrifices I made for you kids. You know how important it is for me to keep the shop open on Sundays."

Inwardly, Erin sighed. "I don't mind having the boys over, you know that. I would just appreciate it if you'd call first, so I can be prepared. Sally's brother just came into town yesterday, so I'm not alone in the house."

"Oh?" Her mother's interest was piqued. "The photographer? I've never met him. Perhaps I should say hello."

"He's not here now, but he'll be staying a while. There will be plenty of time to meet him."

"Will he be staying for Christmas? Perhaps he would like to come along with you kids."

Erin's stomach turned. This was it. The annual Christmas tug of war had begun. They had tried to be fair, to stay with each parent every other Christmas, but neither their mother nor their father could accept that, forcing their children to divide their time equally between the two households, but never making either one of them happy.

"Perhaps Thomas and Sally prefer to stay in their own home this time, as they have a visitor."

"We'll see," her mother replied. "But you will be there, won't you?"

The twins leaned on the car horn, saving Erin from having to reply. Her mother turned around and made an angry gesture at the car. "We'll talk about this later, Erin. Thanks again."

Erin waved to her brothers, then entered the house again. The place seemed so quiet after two days with a couple of noisy little boys. Walking around, she straightened out the mess they had made, then threw herself on the living-room couch. Children were a lot of work, but they were worth every minute. She could hardly wait until she had one of her own.

Tomorrow.

Her stomach clenched in nervous anticipation. Her whole life would change tomorrow.

CHAPTER THREE

HER palms were sweating. Her heart was racing.

And all she was doing was standing outside the clinic.

Resisting the urge to jump back into Sabrina, her faithful red car, drive home and crawl under something, she forced herself to look objectively at the building. It looked cold. All glass and white bricks, but much smaller than she had imagined. She had thought this place would be huge.

Admittedly, storage space in such a facility would not take up much room.

She sighed, breathing out a mushroom of crystallized air, and looked helplessly around. The shops would open in about half an hour, but the streets were still empty. She felt out of place standing there on the corner.

The appointment was half an hour away. She considered driving around, or taking a walk, but decided to go ahead and enter the building. They had to have a waiting room. It would give her a chance to get used to the place.

Squaring her shoulders, she ordered her heart to behave, and pushed open the glass door.

The lobby was silent. White marbled floor, white marbled walls. Large potted plants were the only decoration. Her heels clicking on the hard surface, she walked resolutely to the desk.

"Erin Avery. I have an appointment at ten."

The receptionist couldn't be more than twenty, a black-haired beauty with a wide smile.

"Welcome." She turned to her computer and tapped on the keys. "You're here for an orienting session, right?"

Erin drew her brows together and shrugged. "I suppose so. I've never been here before."

"OK. Well, would you perhaps wait in there?" She pointed to an open door behind her. "I'll be with you at ten precisely."

Erin walked briskly to the waiting room, hoping to hide her anxiety. The chamber was small, but very different from the stark lobby. It was painted in soft blues and pink and children's drawings decorated the walls. She slid into a pastel chair and took a deep calming breath. Her heart was still racing, and showing no signs of slowing down.

To look on the bright side, the waiting room was unoccupied. In her present state, the sight of other clients, or, God forbid, donors, would send her flying out of the nearest exit.

Small tables dotted the floor between the uncomfortable plastic chairs. She picked at random something to read and stared at the text without seeing it. It was difficult to believe that she was actually here. The appointment had been made weeks ago. She had noted it in her diary as ''SB'', and then avoided thinking about it.

Why the anxiety? Why the pounding heart and the sinking feeling? This was what she wanted: this was the way to make her dream come true, her dream of an undivided family. Her dream of happiness. A child that would never be torn between bitterly feuding parents the way she and her brother and sister had been torn apart all their lives.

''Miss Avery?'' Her eyes suddenly focused on the colorful pamphlet showing pictures of smiling women and couples holding their babies. ''Follow me, please.'' It was the young receptionist again. Erin followed her down the long corridor and was finally ushered into an office. To her surprise, the girl followed her inside and shut the door before sitting down at the desk.

Erin noticed she was still holding the pamphlet from the waiting room and stuffed it into a pocket before shrugging off her coat and sitting down. ''I thought I would be seeing the doctor?''

The young woman smiled. ''This is just preliminary work now. My job is to tell you all the facts and explain how you pick a donor, if that is still what you want. After that, we make a new appointment for you with the doctor. She will be able to answer any remaining questions.''

''I see.''

''OK...'' The girl cleared her throat and shuffled some papers around the desk, looking almost as nervous as Erin was. With amusement that almost managed to distract her from her nerves, Erin realized that this was probably a first for both of them.

''Is this the first time you've done this?'' she asked impulsively.

The girl flushed. ''Yes. Our regular interviewer is off sick today.''

"I see."

"But I've watched it many times," she hastened to reassure Erin. "I really know what I'm doing."

"I'm sure you do."

"Oh, and my name is Rachel Bond, by the way." She pointed to the name tag on her blouse.

Rachel got to work, quickly explaining the procedure, but sounding as though she was reading the information aloud. Judging from her lack of eye contact, she probably was. Erin listened patiently. She had already done thorough research using the Internet and there was nothing new in the information presented to her.

Nevertheless, hearing the girl describe the process, using the word "you" in every other sentence, felt far closer—and far more frightening—than reading about it.

Rachel wrapped up her monologue, then fetched what looked like a questionnaire from a drawer.

"OK, next I will ask you some questions to help you determine what kind of a donor you are looking for."

Erin nodded. The girl hesitated, flipped through the few pages and then finally began.

"Do you have specific preferences regarding donor characteristics?"

"Preferences?" Erin repeated hesitantly.

"Hair color, eye color, build, personality?"

She shook her head mutely.

"If you have a picture of the social father, we can try to match his looks."

"Social father," Erin muttered, testing the unfamiliar phrase. "No, there is no social father."

"I see." Rachel kept her voice neutral. "Will there be a second mother?"

"A second moth...?" Erin blinked in confusion, but finally caught on. "Er—no. Just me."

"In that case, many single women prefer a donor whose looks match their own. That way, there is more of a chance that the child will look like their parent."

Erin clenched and unclenched her hands. She was in way over her head. She hadn't thought this far, hadn't realized she could influence her child's characteristics by choosing the particular donor.

The child would not be just hers, she realized for the first time. It never could be. Her child would have half of his or her genes from a stranger. Someone neither of them would ever know. If she had a son, he would never be able to look at his father and see himself reflected in some of his features. She would never have a husband whose features would be a mature version of the tiny sleeping face in the cradle.

Well, that is how you want it, isn't it? she asked herself in annoyance. *You want to do this alone.*

"Who are these men?" she couldn't help asking. "And why do they do this?"

"Most of them are students," the girl replied. "And as to why they do it—there are different reasons. Some like to help infertile couples or single women. Some do it for the token fee they are paid." She leaned forward, and lowered her voice. "If you ask me, a lot of them simply like the idea of a certain type of immortality—knowing that there may be dozens of their offspring roaming the earth."

Erin tried to chuckle, but it came out like a groan. That explanation would fit in with man's supposed innate desire to procreate.

However, it was not what a potential mother wanted to hear. It looked as though Rachel had been sent out into the world without the necessary training in tactfulness.

''How many times is each man's sperm used?''

''In each area, we try to limit it to one child per hundred thousand inhabitants.''

Erin quickly calculated. That would mean ten children in the city. More than she cared to know in this country alone.

Rachel prattled on. ''Some get sent abroad. And of course we can't know if they also donate to other facilities. And then some of the sperm has been donated from abroad.''

Erin shuddered. Her child might have dozens of siblings and would never know them. Hundreds even.

Theoretically, a thousand siblings.

''We pick them very carefully,'' Rachel hastened to add, obviously noticing Erin's sickened pallor. ''Only five to ten per cent of the applicants are accepted as donors. Their physical health, mental health, family history...all these factors are checked as carefully as possible to minimize the risk for mother and child.''

"I see," she managed to croak, her head spinning a bit.

"The danger of sexually transmitted diseases is practically non-existent," Rachel continued, unaware that she was doing a far better job of frightening Erin than reassuring her. "We screen carefully for just about everything. And as for HIV—the sperm is kept in quarantine for six months. If the donor tests positive for HIV at that time, the sperm is naturally thrown away."

Erin wasn't sure she wanted all this information, let alone to hear the word "carefully" one more time. She cleared her throat, then tried to turn her thoughts and the conversation to more positive matters.

"What about…? Could I have two children by the same donor? So that they would be full siblings?"

Rachel nodded, her black pony-tail bobbing. "Of course. Then we would freeze some of the embryos to be used at a later date. Unless you want to try for twins?"

Erin shook her head in confusion.

"Would you like to see the donor menu now?"

Donor menu?

Erin bit her lip, holding back the hysterical giggles that echoed in her brain. This was no time for her zany sense of humor to take control. She *would* stop herself from asking if she could have fries and a cola with that. Not trusting her voice to keep steady, she simply nodded.

The girl stood up and motioned Erin to take her place at the desk. She turned the computer on, clicking rapidly until a white screen with a border of blue and pink roses appeared. ''This is really very simple. Are you familiar with computers?''

Erin nodded.

''Good. It's pretty much self-explanatory. If you have any problems or questions, just click the help button, and I will get a message at my desk and come over. You can stay here and look over your options as long as you like. Or, if you have Internet access at home, you can also access this page from there.'' She handed Erin a small business card with the name of the clinic and a website address. ''When you leave, just make a new appointment at the front desk. I will probably be there, and, if not, someone else will.''

Erin was left in the small office. She was cold. Her hands and feet were icy. Rubbing her hands together, she looked at the baby pictures covering the wall. Hundreds of beautiful little children. Some of them might be her baby's brothers or sisters.

She shook her head. This would not do. The baby would be hers, and hers alone. She would bite the bullet and find the right genes. It wasn't the perfect way, but then this wasn't a perfect world. She would have her baby though. Her very own baby, and nobody else would ever be able to claim it.

She stared at the screen, mechanically clicked a few times at random, then resolutely began reading through the donor list, taking notes as she went along. It involved a lot of statistics for each donor, even personal information such as interests and hobbies.

By noon she had narrowed the list down to five. She wasn't really sure on what basis she had chosen those five. The decision had been made on intuition more than anything else. They didn't even have general looks in common.

She jotted down the identification number for the five men, the five gene donors, she corrected herself, and stuck the note in the envelope that Rachel had left. She would ask the doctor to pick one of those randomly. That way, she wouldn't think of the baby's father as "the computer nerd" or "the musician."

She wasn't going to think about the baby's father at all.

Rachel was still at her desk and accepted Erin's envelope with a smile. "Would you like an appointment with the doctor for further discussion?" she asked.

Erin shook her head. "I don't think that will be necessary," she replied. "I don't really have any further questions. I would like to make an appointment for the procedure itself, though."

The girl's smile widened in satisfaction at a job well done. She consulted a diary. "We could inseminate you in the middle of January. If your cycles are regular, you should be ovulating then. Would that date suit you?"

January? January was ages away. Erin considered asking for a December appointment, but then rejected the idea. She was not rushing into anything. Two more months to think things over would make certain this was the right decision.

If all goes well: an October baby, a calculating voice whispered in her ear, sending goose-bumps along her spine.

"January 14th it is, then." The girl printed out a note and handed it to Erin. "We might contact you before that, after the doctor has gone through your file."

Erin thanked the girl and walked away in a daze. The slip of paper not only indicated the date, but also the price. She carefully tucked it in her wallet behind her driver's license. It was not a high price to pay for a no-strings baby.

Thoughts of the baby filled her thoughts over the next few days. Erin walked around in a daze. As she had afternoon shifts at the library on Tuesday and Wednesday, she didn't see much of her housemate. He was gone when she got up in the morning, and wasn't home when she got back from the library at ten.

She had Friday off. Friday morning saw her sitting in the kitchen in her nightgown, drinking the remnants of the coffee Nathan had made before leaving.

She decided to go on a very special shopping trip.

* * *

The shopping mall was quiet this time of day. Erin walked directly to her destination, her heart picking up speed in a mixture of anticipation and a strange kind of fear. Since Natalie was born she had frequently visited the baby-clothes shop to buy small presents for her niece. She loved choosing the small outfits. But Natalie was almost a year old now, and the clothes on the newborn shelves seemed minuscule in comparison.

Color.

Her hand paused on the tiny hangers. Would it be a boy or a girl? Although she hadn't wanted to choose one or the other, she knew that she wanted to know as soon as the doctors could tell. Ignoring the blue and pink bundles, she reverently ran her hands over tiny white overalls. A green sweater, knitted loosely with a pattern of dark green flowers, caught her eye. Small, so small. Next Christmas, would she really hold a tiny baby of her own in her arms?

"Can I help you?"

Startled, Erin almost dropped the small green sweater, then quickly put it back on the shelf. "No, thank you, I'm just looking," she muttered, smiling almost apologetically. The shop assistant's gaze moved professionally to her flat stomach for a split second before tagging her as a relative instead of a mother-to-be.

"You just let me know."

Erin nodded, then moved away, feeling foolish. What was she doing here? There were still two months until her baby would even be conceived. Still, she lingered in the shop, slowly taking in all the baby paraphernalia.

She would buy something. That would help her to establish her decision, to make it seem real. Something small, yet indicating that soon there would be a tiny new individual in her life. A T-shirt, perhaps. She browsed the T-shirt rack, holding garments that seemed too small even for a doll. All sorts of pictures and phrases decorated them, making her grin as she flipped through them. "I'm the best", "Please change me", "Here comes trouble!"…

She pulled her hand back from the rack as if the material had burnt her.

"I love my daddy".

Oh, God.

The telephone rang again. Erin rolled her eyes as she reluctantly made her way to the phone. She was in a bad mood from her fruitless shopping trip, and for some reason her mood had gone from bad to worse when after only hours at home there had been three phone calls for Nathan. All from women. Three different women, by the sound of it.

She answered in a harsh tone of voice, her thoughts straying to Nathan's intense body language that first evening, how she had been silly enough to interpret it as directed especially towards her. But she was obviously just one of the crowd.

Not that she wanted it any other way. She didn't want a man in her life. Not ever, and especially not now.

It was another one of those silky, sexy female voices, asking for Nathan by his first name. Erin could just picture the long legs and flowing blond hair. She ran her fingers through her own reddish hair and stared ruefully into the mirror at her five-foot-four frame.

"No, I'm sorry, Nathan isn't here."

She had offered to take messages so far, and there were three names and numbers on the pad by the phone, each one scribbled more forcefully than the last one. She decided not to offer this time.

"Oh. Are you his sister?"

"No…I'm… No, I'm not his sister. I'm definitely not his sister."

Erin stared aghast at herself in the mirror. Where had those last words come from, spoken in that insinuating tone full of shared secrets?

There must be a little devil hidden inside her as well.

The woman was silent for a moment. "I see. Would you tell him, then, that Rosemary said hello?"

"No problem," Erin muttered, already feeling foolish. How would Nathan react if he found out she had been masquerading as his live-in lover?

She spent the rest of the evening in front of the television, with the phone unplugged. She was not about to become that man's answering service, especially not when she was likely to make a fool out of herself in the process.

At about eleven she heard Nathan come in. As she heard him enter the living room she called over her shoulder, "You have messages from Rosemary, Evelyn, Sylvie, and Mary. Just how large is your harem and do they all have a 'y' in their name?"

When there was no answer, she looked around, to see Nathan standing next to a woman who was looking at him with one elegant eyebrow raised.

Nathan stared at her, then displayed a forced smile to his companion. "This is Erin, the woman I told you was staying here," he explained to her. "Erin, this is Linda."

Erin smiled sweetly. The woman was all legs and silky hair, just as she had imagined upon speaking to Nathan's girlfriends on the phone. "Pleased to meet you. That's Lynda with a 'y', I presume?"

"Erin…" Nathan growled, making her feel like a naughty child.

"Nice to meet you, Erin. Actually, it's simply an 'i'." The woman smiled politely and nodded at Erin, then turned to Nathan. "It's getting late. Perhaps you could just get the papers and then I'll be on my way." The woman's voice matched her refined looks, but it was laced with a subtle tone of irritation.

Erin found it wisest to turn her attention back to the loud sitcom playing on the television screen. She stuffed some popcorn into her mouth, and tried to ignore the unpleasant feeling of knowing she'd done something wrong.

She had been inexcusably rude to that woman. On the other hand, she thought, her mood lifting slightly, she might just have saved the poor woman from heartbreak. And as for Nathan, he could just get a hotel room if he couldn't control his urges. His sister's home was no place to be dragging women in for casual sex.

Lynda, or, rather, Linda left by herself, leaving Erin to face Nathan. She sank deeper in the couch. There were bound to be some consequences of her actions. With dread she listened to the sound of his footsteps approaching.

Nathan grabbed the remote control off the table and muted the sound. Then he lifted her legs to make space for himself on the couch, and sat down, holding her bare feet in his lap.

''Well, Miss Librarian. Want to tell me what that was all about?''

Erin tried to pull her feet back, but he didn't let go. In fact, his thumbs were stroking her ankles in a way that sent all sorts of sensations shooting up her legs. She glanced at his face, seeing the half-smile that never indicated anything about his mood. His voice was cool, almost amused.

She couldn't figure him out.

"You have no business bringing women here for sex!" she blurted out.

He raised an eyebrow. "My sex life is none of your concern." He tightened his grip on her ankles. "Unless you would like to participate, of course?"

Anger gave her the strength to pull her feet from his grasp. She scooted up in one corner of the couch, arms around her knees. "No, thanks," she spat out. "I don't want used merchandise."

Nathan nodded thoughtfully. "I see. No used merchandise. That might make things somewhat difficult for you."

The man was impossible. "I mean I wouldn't want to 'participate' with someone who is already seeing at least five women."

"Ah, so we're counting," he murmured. "You sound jealous."

Horrified, Erin realized that was exactly how she sounded.

"Come here, Librarian." He grabbed her forearms and somehow managed to move her into his lap. "It's OK to like me, you know. I like you too." He put his hands on each side of her face, forcing her to meet his gaze.

This wasn't right. He was supposed to be angry at her rude interference in his love life; not all understanding and sympathetic over her jealousy. She couldn't even accuse him of arrogance. She read his signals; he read hers.

That didn't mean she had to admit that he was right.

"I don't like you," she tried to protest, hitting his shoulder half-heartedly with a fist. God, it felt good to be in his arms. "I don't like you at all."

"Yes, you do." He feathered her cheeks and nose with small, teasing nibbles, making her lips tingle in anticipation of a kiss that never came. "You don't want to like me, but you do."

In a burst of sensual energy, her hands, held against his chest in a feeble effort to hold him away, all of a sudden transmitted to her brain the warmth of his body and the subtle strength of his muscles. She snatched her hands back and tried to scramble out of his arms. Her reward was an even tighter prison, as he held her on his lap with one arm under her knees, the other under her shoulders, hands locked together. His smile revealed tiny dimples in his cheeks; the green eyes shimmered in the faint glow from the television. Her fingers itched to touch his face and bury themselves in his thick hair. Instead, she curled them into tight fists, outraged at the helpless response of her body and very much aware that she wasn't exactly fighting to be released.

''One tiny experiment, Erin, then I'll let you go.''

She had a pretty good idea what the experiment entailed. Red curls danced around her face as she shook her head wildly.

''Just one kiss. Nothing more.'' He grinned down at her. ''I promise to resist any advances you might make in the throes of passion.''

Her lips tingled. She did want to kiss him, to find out if it would be anything like her disturbing dream kisses. Staring into his eyes, the warm green embers framed by dark lashes, she felt an urge to touch him, to possess him, to absorb the warmth of him. With a hint of surprise she realized that she trusted him to keep his word and not push for more than just a kiss.

And she so wanted that kiss. What harm could one kiss possibly do?

Nathan's gaze lowered, and he blew a soft stream of air onto her lips, which parted automatically, eager to receive his breath.

"Go ahead, Librarian," he whispered. "Kiss me."

Without volition, her hands unclenched. They ran up his chest, trailed over his neck and into the warmth of his hair. His eyes turned a deeper shade of green as she pulled his head down, and when she touched her lips to his, she felt them curve in a smile. Somehow, that didn't matter. He could laugh all he wanted. He had offered; she would accept.

He let her set the pace. Enjoying her freedom, she experimented, played with him, nibbling at his lips and darting her tongue out to lick at them. When she felt the warm gust of his breath between his lips she deepened the kiss, and lost herself immediately in the pleasure of his enthusiastic response.

He was the one to break it off.

She came to her senses to find their bodies as tight together as humanly possible, her arms wound around his neck and her tingling breasts pressed against his chest. One of his hands was in her hair, the other on her back, holding her against him. Her own hands were equally busy: one buried in his hair, the other cupped around the slightly abrasive curve of his jaw. Her whole body was trembling, and after a while she realized that so was his.

He rested his forehead against hers as they both tried to contain their breathing. With every breath, she drew in his scent; felt the warm gust of his own rapid breaths on her cheek. That did nothing to calm her racing heart.

Mistake! the sensible part of her brain shouted. It was time to remove herself from his embrace and set some ground rules.

In just a few seconds.

"I think the experiment is a success," he muttered at last, moving his lips against her cheek. "Wouldn't you agree?"

"That would depend upon the experimental goal and on your definition of success," she croaked. She kept her eyes closed, not sure she would ever be ready to face either Nathan or the rest of the world again.

Nathan chuckled. His eyelashes brushed against her brow and, even as she shuddered at the strangely erotic contact, she knew his eyes were open. Reluctantly she opened her own, seeing him once again look at her with that enigmatic gaze that took in everything and revealed nothing.

"We've established that we...like...each other," he said. "The question is, where do we go from here?"

"Where?" she managed to ask. "What do you mean, where? Your bed or mine?" She strained to keep her voice sarcastic but suspected she had failed abysmally.

"That's one possibility," he murmured. "Although I wasn't necessarily planning on moving that fast." He grinned, stroking her cheek with a finger. "Are you inviting me?"

Her face beet-red, Erin scrambled out of his arms again, irritated to be behaving like a neurotic virgin but unable to help herself.

Was he serious? She couldn't believe he expected her to instantly jump into bed with him after one kiss.

That she was tempted was completely beside the point.

"However enjoyable kissing you may be, Nathan, I think we should keep this simple." Her voice was unsteady and she cleared her throat and ran a shaking hand through her mussed hair. Play it cool and sophisticated, yet firm. She'd have to bluff him into thinking she was just as experienced at this game as he was. "You're probably a good lover and all and I like sex as much as the next woman, but I'm not about to go to bed with you. Not now, not ever."

Oh, God. That did *not* sound cool and sophisticated. His lips quirked in a badly concealed smile and she felt like fleeing from the room and hiding under something. Cool and sophisticated had morphed into naïve and childish.

It wasn't much of a consolation, but at least her face couldn't possibly turn a deeper shade of red.

"I see," he murmured, grinning up at her. "No going to bed. How about just petting on the sofa, then?"

"Was that what you had in mind when you agreed to live here with me? I thought you just wanted to play Scrabble and talk about books! Remember? You wanted a civil relationship without flirting!"

Nathan leaned forward as he looked up at her.

"I didn't think I'd be lusting after you!" he almost growled. "When I'm interested in a woman, I flirt with her. Force of habit, I'm afraid. It's a message. It means: Hi, I'm interested, are you? What follows after that is up to her.''

Silence.

She stared at him, aghast.

Nathan reached towards her, grabbing both her hands in one of his. ''Erin, don't over-analyze. Why don't we just take things as they come and see where this leads to?''

''I know where it leads to!'' she shouted as she pulled her hands free of his warm grasp. ''Your bed, that's where!''

He nodded. ''If things work out. What's wrong with that?''

Transfixed, she could only look as he reached again towards her, touching her hand, enveloping it in his own before pulling her down next to him again. His thumb stroked her palm and she gasped as the simple touch sent flashes of fire along her nerves. He smiled, a slow, predatory smile, accurately gauging her reactions. Nevertheless, she couldn't find the strength to pull her hand away.

''We'll be good together,'' he murmured, his eyes intent on her face. His arrogant presumption startled her into action. She jumped to her feet, snatching her hand from his grasp.

Folding her arms on her chest, she opened her mouth, then closed it again when she realized she had no idea what she was going to say. Without speaking, she turned on her heel and retreated to her room.

After tossing and turning all night, by morning she had made up her mind. She would have to leave. There was no alternative: she couldn't continue to stay in this house with Nathan. All her plans, everything she wanted in life was in danger because she couldn't trust herself around him.

Feeling like a coward, she sneaked out of the house without even her morning coffee, and was relieved to find him gone in the afternoon when she returned from a day spent randomly touring the city, visiting friends and window-shopping.

Her sister answered on the first ring.

"Erika, I know you're cramped for space, but could I stay with you for a few days?"

"With me? What happened? Aren't you at Thomas's house?"

Erin leaned her head back and closed her eyes, fighting back a headache creeping along her temples. "It's a long story, sis. Sally's brother is here, and I don't want to stay here alone with him.''

''Saint Nathan?'' Erika's tone darkened. ''Why? Is he a creep?''

''No! Not at all. We are... I just... I don't... He's...'' Erin gave up and shut her mouth. It was probably wisest just to stop talking.

''Aha,'' said her sister, reading her feelings accurately as ever. ''So you're falling for Saint Nathan?''

Wrapping the telephone cord around her fingers, Erin shook her head. ''Please, don't interrogate me about him, I'm confused enough as it is.''

Her sister squealed. ''Terrific! It's about time a man did that to you. Just a moment.''

Erin rolled her eyes at the pause, which she knew meant her sister was changing phones, getting comfortable for a long interrogation about the state of her love life.

Abruptly, Erika's voice echoed again through the phone. ''Tell me all about it. Have you been to bed yet?''

''That's none of your business!'' Erin said firmly, while knowing her sister would drag every detail out of her sooner or later.

''Is he a good kisser?''

Erin's mind instantly replayed their one and only kiss, but she didn't realize she had made a sound until Erika's knowing laughter bubbled from the phone. "That sigh says it all, sis! What else?"

She might as well come clean. "Nothing else, Erika," she confessed with resignation. "It was just the one kiss."

"That must have been one hell of a kiss," Erika speculated. "One kiss and you're running away in panic?"

A tell-tale crackle buzzed through the phone. "Erika, are you settling down with a snack while interrogating me about my sex life?"

"I can't interrogate you about your sex life because you don't have one," Erika retorted, mouth obviously full. "But things seem to be perking up. No pun intended. Tell me more. What was the context of that kiss?"

"Context?"

"You know. Did he just grab you suddenly and kiss you senseless, or did you have a cuddle in the back of the cinema, or did he kiss you goodbye after a date?"

"Um…actually, I kissed him." Why was she telling her sister this?

There was a momentary silence on the other end of the line. "*You* kissed *him?*"

"Kind of," Erin confessed, wrapping the cord around her fingers as she felt her face warm.

"Way to go, sis!" Erika squealed. "Finally you're coming to your senses. I'm proud of you!"

Erin moved the receiver to the other ear and pressed a hand to her hot cheek. "To get back to my reason for calling—"

"Are you sure you should be running away? I bet things could get interesting. Why don't you stick around and see what happens?"

"Because I know what will happen if I stay!" Erin burst out, repeating what she had told Nathan. "I know it and he knows it, and I'm not about to let that happen!"

"What's he like?"

"He's..." Words failed her. "I don't know."

"Good-looking? Smart? Funny? Charming? Sexy?"

"Er—yes."

Erika giggled. "All of the above? You're in deep, sis. Sounds like you've already lost your heart."

Irritation began to mount. Erin ignored the voice asking if Erika had perhaps hit too close to home. "Erika, stop it. Can I stay with you?"

"Sure. If Nathan really is such a hunk, maybe I should trade places with you."

Erin frowned in consternation. "Aren't you still seeing Richard?"

"Kind of. It's not serious. But don't worry, I wouldn't make a move on your Nathan without your full approval."

Another thought occurred to Erin. "Is it a bad time to have me staying, Erika?"

"Of course not," her sister replied breezily. "No problem. We'll just go to his place if we want privacy."

Taking advantage of her sister's visual absence, Erin rolled her eyes. Her twin's casual attitude towards sex was still a mystery to her. The sisters had reacted to their family issues by going in two different directions. The end result was the same, of course. No one close enough to hurt. While Erin had shied away from any close relationships with men, Erika jumped from one superficial relationship to another, pushing her boyfriends away if they seemed about to get closer. She had been seeing her current boyfriend for a year, which was a record, but neither Thomas nor Erin had even seen him. Rarely did she mention him at all.

"Come any time, sis."

Erin packed slowly, often stopping in mid-action while she pondered through some stubborn thoughts. All of a sudden, life had become confusing.

She had never really stopped to analyze her attitude towards men and relationships. From the time she was a little girl, she'd known it wasn't for her, wasn't worth the risk of so much pain and trouble. Then later, Tom and Sally had shown her close up that love was possible, happiness was possible. Family life could be positive and warm. They had given her the courage to try for a relationship of her own. That disaster was something she tried not to think about, something that had proven once and for all that it would not work out. Not for her. Perhaps it was her own fault, for being such a poor judge of character, allowing herself to be used by someone who didn't think twice about casting her aside when she was no longer convenient for him. That experience had convinced her that relationships were first and foremost a trap, an obstacle to happiness.

At the other end of the spectrum, the emptiness of her sister's life, jumping from one frivolous relationship to another, had always deterred her from having an intimate relationship without the threat of a commitment or a future. Neither option was worth all the pain and bother. Independence and celibacy were the only options she had, if she wanted a secure and stable future. Nothing could be worth risking a repeat of her parents' story, or her own disastrous relationship.

But she did want a child. After little Natalie was born, that feeling had become stronger. Although never thinking it completely through, she had always imagined she would raise the child by herself, with the father not even a distant figure in the child's life.

The idea of having a fling with Nathan had popped up during the sleepless night. To allow herself a fling with him, to disregard the effect that would have upon her brother and his family. For one moment she even contemplated the crazy idea of deliberately making love with him hoping to create a baby for her to raise. Nathan had all the qualities she could wish for in a genetic father, plus he would soon be going away again.

But it would never work. She didn't want anyone stepping forward to claim paternity over her child. Nathan was too close to the family, he would know about the child. She wanted the father completely out of the picture. Luckily, she lived in a time where such a possibility existed.

She finished packing, then glanced around the room to see if she was forgetting something. Nothing of her personal belongings remained, except for the huge fish tank, and there was no space for that in her sister's small apartment. She would leave Nathan a note and ask him to feed the fish.

Dear Nathan.

She paused, tapping the pencil against the paper.

I will be staying with my sister Erika for a while. I would appreciate it if you could feed my fish once a day. The food is in my room on the table next to the fish tank.
Thank you very much.
Erin

She tapped the glass of the fish tank with a fingernail, whispering to Your Boyfriend and

Your Girlfriend, "I'll be back to get you as soon as I can." Then she picked up her bags and walked out onto the landing, holding the note between her teeth. She would leave it on the refrigerator under a magnet.

"What the hell do you think you're doing?"

She jumped at his harsh tone, then glared back at the threatening figure on the stairs. He was on his way up, his hair tousled from the wind. It reminded her uncomfortably of the way he had looked framed by the window at their first meeting.

"What does it look like I'm doing?" she asked back, allowing the note to drop from her mouth and flutter to the floor.

"It looks like you're leaving," he said, advancing towards her and picking the note up. Seeing his name on it, he flipped it open and read her short message. His scowl deepened.

"Bingo, Holmes." She dropped her luggage and took refuge behind it, feeling moderately safer with the cases between them.

"Because of me?"

She hesitated, but it seemed pointless to deny it. The reason was obvious and his remark had been more of a statement than a

question. ''I can't stay, Nathan, I'm sorry.''
She picked up her cases again and started
down the stairs.

A heavy hand descended on her shoulder.
''Wait. Let's talk about this.'' She carried de-
terminedly on down the stairs.

''Erin. I mean it. Let's talk.''

''I'm not sleeping with you,'' she blurted
out, pivoting around to face him. ''No sex, no
kisses, no flirting. Nothing.''

Standing one step above her, he blinked.
''OK.''

She nodded, relieved this was so easy. She
relaxed too soon. Nathan sat down on the
stairs, pulling her hand until she sat down too.

''What's this all about? I would never force
myself on you, Erin.''

''I know,'' she muttered. ''It's not that I'm
afraid that you would. It's my own fault. There
is this tension between us, but it's just not
meant to be.''

''Tell me why.'' He was still holding on to
her hand.

''I don't have to give you a reason why I
don't want to sleep with you,'' she snapped.

''No. But I would like to know why you
won't give us a chance.''

The gentleness of his voice was her undoing. Erin blinked back tears. It would be so easy to allow him close, to let things happen.

But the price was too high.

"Oh, no, you're crying."

The panic in his voice drew a chuckle out of her. "Don't worry, I won't melt. You must have seen women cry before."

"Not many," he muttered. "I prefer to make them laugh." He pulled her head to his chest, shaking her lightly when she resisted. "Don't worry, I'm in friends mode. No seduction is imminent."

She allowed herself to relax against him, enjoying the warmth of him, his scent and the safe feeling of his arms around her. It didn't matter that they were sitting in an awkward position on the stairs, her bags strewn around them.

"Tell me what's spooking you."

Erin closed her eyes, giving in to his gently authoritative voice. She might as well tell him some of the background for the way she was. Some of the reasons why there was no sense in them even considering having a relationship, even if either of them were the relationship type, and even if she would ever again take that kind of a risk.

"There are a million reasons, Nathan. For example, if we have a…a fling, or something, it will eventually hurt Sally and Thomas."

Nathan continued to stroke her hair and she couldn't summon the strength to sit up.

"How could that possibly hurt them?"

Erin shook her head and pushed her face closer into his sweater. Was the man completely ignorant of family subtleties? "You know," she mumbled into his chest. "After it ended, we'd be ignoring each other, you wouldn't want to stay for Christmas if I was there, I wouldn't want to babysit Natalie because she talked about you all the time, Sally and Thomas would try to figure out ways to include both of us without hurting our feelings…" She sighed. "It would just be one giant mess."

"I think you're overreacting, but it sounds like you've been there before," he murmured.

"I have," she said. "And so has Thomas. I would never want to put my brother through what my family goes through just to keep our parents from wringing each other's necks."

"I'm sorry."

Erin shrugged. "We live with it. At Thomas's wedding, I kept Dad busy on one side of the room, while Erika handled Mom on the other side."

"What happened between your mother and your father?"

"Just life, I guess. They had three kids in two years and they were only seventeen when Thomas was born. Neither of them could really handle it. Both did a lot of things that hurt the other."

"I see."

Erin was silent for a while, lost in thought.

"But to get back to us..."

Erin pulled her head back, just far enough to glare at him.

"The hypothetical us," he amended. "You must see that it would be a totally different situation? And," he added, "frankly, I can't imagine ever wanting to wring your neck. It's just too kissable."

Before she knew what had happened he was already drawing back, but she felt the imprint of warm lips on her neck.

"Why do you keep doing that to me?" she asked, childishly rubbing the kiss away with her hand.

"Doing what?"

"Making me..." She stopped herself before she could finish the sentence. *Want you,* she silently added.

He was reading her mind again, she just knew it. She could see it in the wicked smile hovering on his lips, deepening the laughter lines around his eyes.

"Anyway, Nathan, nothing is going to happen between us. If the only way I can ensure that is by leaving, I will. I can stay with Erika."

Nathan shook his head. "You can't go. Sally will never forgive me if she finds out I drove you out of the house."

"Don't be ridiculous," she scoffed. "Sally thinks you're second only to God."

Nathan sighed. "If you really can't stand living with me, I'll leave. You're the one who's house-sitting."

She shook her head, adamant. "If you're worried about her reaction if I leave, what do you think will happen if I'm the one to drive Saint Nathan out of the house?"

"Erin, please. The plants. Eviction of her sister-in-law and the brutal murder of her plants will topple even the mighty Big Brother off his pedestal." He spread his fingers under her nose. "See? Not even a tinge of green. I've been there. Usually I water too much and drown them. When I try to restrain myself, they end up dry and wilting."

His pathetic-little-boy look was just too much. A smile teased at the corner of her mouth and grew into a fully fledged grin when he added in a miserable tone of voice, "And the cactuses are just plain lethal!

"So you'll stay?" he asked, lulled by her smile.

"No."

His face fell and she giggled, brushing the last tears away with the back of her hand.

"You are so manipulative, Nathan. Does that really work on women?"

His mouth opened, then closed. Recovering, he chuckled.

"Guilty as charged," he muttered, running a hand through his hair. "I'm fast running out of tricks, Erin. Help me out, will you? If you really don't feel comfortable staying here with me then I'll leave. It's the logical thing to do. On the other hand, if you'll allow me to stay, I can promise not to treat you in any way different than I do my kid sister.'' He crossed his heart. ''Scouts' honor.''

''I think you're mixing up 'Scouts' honor' and 'Cross my heart and hope to die','' she commented irrelevantly.

He shrugged. ''It's been a very long time since I was a kid.''

Erin hesitated. It would solve a lot of issues if he could promise to keep their relationship platonic. After all, if he tended to stick around this time, to spend time with Sally and Natalie, they might be running into each other a lot from now on.

She made a quick decision to give it a try.

''OK, from now on I'm just your kid sister. Agreed?''

''Agreed,'' he said solemnly, ''but I have one condition of my own.''

''Now, why does that not surprise me?'' she muttered to nobody in particular. Nathan's eyes were glittering with something she wasn't sure she liked.

''It's only good for one week at a time. Friday evening the contract expires and we call a meeting and decide whether to renew it.''

She pondered the matter for a minute, not trusting him one bit.

"What do you mean, renew it?"

"We review the events of the week, and discuss if the premises of the contract have in any way changed in a fashion that warrants a re-evaluation of its goals and directives."

She gave him a suspicious look. "Where did you study law?"

Nathan chuckled. "Just sign on the dotted line."

Erin stared at him for a moment, then shrugged. How much harm could agreeing to that do? All she had to do was to state every week that she wanted to renew their contract. "OK. Agreed."

Peering warily at his victorious grin, she took his hand when he held it out, then almost gasped when his warmth enveloped her palm, his fingers strong and sure as they curved around her hand. "We certainly do a lot of shaking hands," she mumbled. He lifted her hand up to his mouth and dropped a gentle kiss on her knuckles. She snatched it back as if his lips had burned her skin.

"I wasn't complaining! Shaking will do fine," she muttered, rubbing the back of her hand against her jeans as if to eradicate his kiss. One look at the satisfied smile in his eyes and she was having second thoughts. A series of delicious yet forbidden tingles snaked down her spine as she stared almost spellbound up at him. Perhaps this renegotiation idea wasn't such a harmless one after all.

In fact, she was pretty sure she was in deep, deep trouble.

CHAPTER FOUR

IT WAS Friday. That was the first thought in her mind as she slowly emerged from sleep, face buried in the downy pillow. Friday. Nathan's designated renegotiation day. It was also her day off, which was why the alarm clock hadn't woken her up; she worked Saturday instead.

She rolled over onto her back and stared up at the ceiling. A feeling she couldn't identify was clouding her thoughts. She had been waiting for this day; a part of her had anticipated it with excitement, another part had dreaded it.

He really had been on his best behavior all week. In fact, she could almost feel a tentative friendship growing between them. How could that be happening?

It was hard to believe that the grinning devil who had her in stitches with his insightful comic remarks, the sensitive man who'd dried her tears on the stairs, the sophisticated, self-confident man she saw leaving every morning—that this was Nathan Chase, the man she

109

had despised for three years. She shook her head in confusion. There had to be some explanation for the way he had treated his family. There had to be.

She just couldn't figure a way to find out.

Again, her mind strayed to their one kiss, and with a shiver she pulled the covers over her head, wondering what the day might bring. Although there had been plenty of friendly banter over the morning coffee or the late-night news, not one look, word or touch had been out of place. She was curious to know what his renegotiations would entail. Would he even remember his suggestion at all?

She frowned and pulled the covers down to gaze at the ceiling once more. He still had people calling him all the time, half of them women. None of them had come to the house all week and he had been home every night, but she had no idea what he was up to out of the house during the day.

Lost in thought, it was several minutes until she noticed the unusually bright light filtering in through the curtains. Curious, she kicked the covers aside and stretched, then padded barefoot to the window and pulled the blue curtains aside.

Snow!

Finally! Erin jumped up and down in excitement, all thoughts of Nathan forgotten. The first snow of the winter had piled down during the night, covering the garden with a soft white blanket. Stray flakes were still falling. Running downstairs, excited as a child, she shovelled in a quick breakfast before digging to the back of the closet for Sally's ski outfit.

Outside, the snow was as perfect as it had looked from her bedroom window. Moist and thick, perfect to play in, perfect to build snowmen and fortresses. And the weather was perfect too, no wind and not too cold. She laughed aloud as she began playing in the snow, knowing she was being childish and silly, and loving every minute of it.

In due time, a bulky snowman was joined in holy matrimony with a matronly snowwoman, and Erin painstakingly wrapped yellowed straws around their fingers to signify their union. And so came the children. Three little sprites, chasing each other, and a baby in the mother's arms, a tiny snowbaby.

There!

She stepped back to examine her handiwork and saw that it was good.

Time to make some angels in the snow.

She was making her third angel, staring up at the wispy clouds, when she heard the front door open. Turning her head, she saw Nathan emerging, wearing his usual black jeans and a leather jacket, with gloves and scarf as a concession to the cold and the snow.

"Good morning!" she said, smiling. She was not going to be embarrassed about her playing urge. The world would be a better place if more adults took the time to play.

Nathan stared down at her, a big grin appearing by degrees. "You're wearing a snowsuit!" he said in delighted amazement. Erin looked down at herself.

"Actually, it's Sally's. She wears it skiing. Red isn't my color."

He crouched down and offered his hands. She allowed him to pull her up to a sitting position, meeting his eyes as he stared at her with an amazed look on his face.

"You have snowflakes on your lashes. And your cheeks are red." He laughed. "You are full of surprises, Miss Librarian. I don't think I've ever seen an adult playing in the snow before. Not without several kids around, anyway."

Erin shrugged. "You should try it yourself," she said. "It's so much fun! I've never understood why you can't play in the snow any more just because you're over eighteen!"

Nathan smiled. His hands went to her cheeks, warming them. His breath crystallized the air between them. Then his warm lips brushed against her cold ones.

The whisper of a kiss lasted only a few seconds and was interrupted by an amused female voice.

"A most romantic scene, Nathan. Dare I interrupt?"

Over his shoulder, Erin could see the woman sitting inside a car purring in the driveway. A blond, of course.

"One of your babes?" she asked, her lips still almost touching his.

With a small curse, Nathan rose to his feet and joined the woman in the car. They spoke only for a moment, and then the woman drove off without him, leaving him staring at Erin with an unreadable expression.

"You do like blonds, don't you?" she asked with a straight face and climbed somewhat gracelessly to her feet. Movement was not exactly elegant while wearing the heavy snowsuit. What was it with Nathan and these women? Girlfriends? Lovers? Colleagues? She almost stomped her foot in frustration. She needed to know if he was throwing earth-shattering kisses left and right, or if she had been singled out for the honor. But how could she ask him? ''If we're still keeping count, that's babe number six.''

Nathan grinned. ''She counts as a babe, but she's not one of mine.'' He cocked his head to the side. ''Not any more, at least. Well, Miss Librarian, that's three women you have managed to alienate from me in one week.''

She gasped at this unfair accusation, while stowing away his words for later scrutiny. *Not one of mine.* The teasing light in his eyes seemed to back up his words.

She'd have to figure out a way to ask him about those women.

''Me? Who kissed whom? You can't blame me for it this time!''

''Oh, yes, I can,'' he said, his voice a seductive rumble. ''You're the one who manages to look so delectably sexy in that shapeless outfit.''

She looked down at herself. He thought she looked sexy in the red overalls that didn't even show a hint of a waist or the curve of a breast? She was torn between disbelief and smugness.

"How can you possibly find this outfit sexy?"

"I didn't say the outfit looked sexy. I said you did."

She looked away before he did, seeing from the corner of her eye that he continued looking at her for a long minute before turning his attention to her creations in the snow. Erin bit her lip. Perhaps she was a little bit too childish.

"I notice a distinct lack of a halo for your angels," he commented. He knelt down in the snow, disregarding her warning that he would soak his jeans. He reached out with a gloved hand and drew in the snow. "Which is not surprising, all things considered," he continued. "I think this is more appropriate."

Erin watched, chagrined, as he added horns and a pointed tail to her angel. He slapped his hands together to rid them of residual snow and grinned at her. "Well, what do you think? Fitting, isn't it?"

His hair was glittering with tiny snowflakes. Inside her mittens she curled her fingers into fists to prevent them from reaching out to brush the sparkling ice away. Her fingers were actually tingling. Did the man have magnets in his hair?

"You don't seem too upset. Are there plenty more blonds where they came from?"

Nathan's grin got wider. "As a matter of fact, I'm all out of blonds. And you owe me, Miss Librarian. I am a stranger around here. As you have ruined my chances of a blonde guide around town, I'll have to make do with a red-haired one."

"I'll buy you a map."

His eyes sparked with amusement. "I'll let you drive my car."

She hesitated. How did he know about her secret and rather uncharacteristic passion for cars? She'd been eyeing his black sports car with utter envy. She'd even run her fingers over the hood once or twice, but she didn't think he'd ever been around to witness her adoration.

Too late she noticed that he had raked together some snow and already had five nicely packed snowballs ready. Her eyes flew to his face, taking in the wicked smile. In one swift movement she grabbed four of his snowballs and jumped to a safe distance before turning around and bombarding him.

Not one missed. She still had it, the unerring aim that had made her snow-fight enemy number one in her neighbourhood. Cackling gleefully, she ducked behind a tree, scooping up more snow.

"How low can you go, Librarian?" Nathan shouted. "Those were *my* snowballs!"

She emerged from behind the tree, a snowball in each hand. But he was closer than she had anticipated. As she turned around to run away, he grabbed her arm, and she ended up face down in the snow.

Laughing, he grabbed her around the waist and easily turned her around before bracing himself above her. "Gotcha." His voice was low and intimate, his face only inches from hers. With slow, deliberate movements he kissed the snow away from her face.

Erin's giggles slowly subsided and a feeling other than mirth took over. His tousled hair was hanging down and, unable to resist it any longer, she reached up a mittened hand to brush it away. He smiled at the tender gesture, and when she came to her senses and half-heartedly pushed at his shoulder he took her wrists and pinned them above her head.

"Are you going to admit you like me, Librarian?"

"What happens if I do?"

Nathan shrugged, the movement shaking some snow from his hair and onto her forehead and cheeks. He lowered his head and licked the cold wetness away. His tongue was warm, and Erin's shudder had nothing to do with the cold ground pressing against her back.

"I don't know. There are all kinds of possibilities." His words were muffled on account of his lips now enclosing her earlobe. "There are chaste ones, such as going out to dinner tonight, or having a real date tomorrow. Then there are the interesting ones." He paused, pulling his head back to look into her eyes before continuing. "We could make passionate love in the snow, and then spend Christmas recuperating from frostbite." He traced kisses from her ear to the edge of her mouth, then rubbed his nose against hers. The laughter in his eyes was irresistible as his tongue snaked out again to catch a stray snowflake that had landed on her cheek. "We could go inside, light a fire, and check every inch of each other for snow…"

Oh, God.

"We could—"

His next suggestion was interrupted by the distant blow of a car horn from the road, jolting her back to reality. She shook her head to clear it of remaining cobwebs.

Status report: she was lying on her back in the snow, with a man on top of her.

The strangest things kept happening to her since Nathan's arrival. None of them were compatible with the goals she had set for herself, the life she had all planned out.

As if sensing her change of mood, Nathan moved off her to lie on his side in the snow next to her, head propped up on one arm. Something tugged at her heart as his eyes sparkled at her, lashes dewed with snow, but she pushed the feeling away.

"So, how about being my guide?" He reached inside his coat pocket and jiggled his keys above her face. "I've seen the way you look at my car, Librarian. It almost makes me jealous. Drop me off downtown, pick me up for dinner at six and you can keep the car today."

She had to ask.

"What's with all the women?" she blurted out before she could regret it.

"All the women?"

Gesturing angrily while lying on her back in the snow was a challenge, but she did it. "All the 'y' women. And the woman who was here just now. Your harem."

Nathan just grinned. "Are you jealous again?"

That did it. Grabbing a handful of snow, she tugged at his scarf and the sweater underneath, stuffing the wetness down to his chest.

Nathan gasped with shock and dropped his keys, then cursed a blue streak while he tried to fish most of the snow back out. "You were an impossible tomboy, weren't you?" he accused her, throwing a leg over hers when she meant to scramble to her feet. "Wait, Erin, let me answer."

Grudgingly she stilled and waited for his answer.

"There is no harem. The people, men and women, who have been calling me recently are friends and colleagues. That's all. They're working on opening an advertising agency. I've been helping out."

Erin stared at him. She had her answer, but she still wanted his reaffirmation.

"So you're not involved with anyone?"

"Nope."

There was the familiar mixture of relief and dread. He wasn't attached. Not that it mattered. Or perhaps it did. Perhaps it meant she could indulge in one more intoxicating kiss without feeling guilty.

No. It would have simplified things if he had been involved. She had her baby to think about.

"Nathan…?"

"Yes?" The warmth in his eyes was almost unbearable.

"Nothing has changed. I shouldn't have asked, it was none of my business and I don't want to be a tease. We shouldn't have these Friday negotiations because nothing will happen… I mean, I wanted to know if you were kissing me while involved with someone else, but that doesn't mean I want us to get together or anything…"

He only smiled at her incoherent ramblings, then dug through the snow for his car keys. He dangled them in front of her again. "What do you say? Borrow my car today, be my guide tonight?"

She took her cue from the carefree smile crooking his lips. She had told him her terms.

He knew the score. Why not allow life to be simple for a little while and enjoy his company while it lasted? Obviously, that was what he intended to do.

And anyway, when would she again be given the chance to drive such a gorgeous car?

Giving in to temptation, she grabbed the keys and jumped to her feet. ''You've got a deal.''

His arm went around her shoulder as they walked back to the house. Nathan stopped as he saw her snow people clustered by the front door.

''Snowbabies,'' he said with a chuckle. ''A whole snow family. Do you want this many kids?''

Erin smiled wistfully. ''Maybe not four. Perhaps two or three. At least one, that's for sure.''

''Why aren't you a wife and mother yet, Librarian?''

''Guess I just haven't got around to it yet.''

''Never met the right man?''

She shrugged. ''I don't believe in Mr Right.''

''I see.'' Nathan removed his gloves and ran his fingers over the face of the smallest snowbaby, sculpting and shaping. Erin watched with amazement as he magically created the curve of an ear and cheek where only lumps of snow had existed before. It looked as though Nathan was capable of artistic creativity even without a photographic lens. "A romantic cynic?"

"I'm not romantic."

"Yes, you are," he murmured. "You create snow families, you light scented candles, you eat chocolate with a look of pure ecstasy and, last but not least, you kiss like an angel. You're a romantic." He put a cold finger to her cheek and made her look at him. "So are you going to have your three children with Mr Good-Enough? Or even Mr Wrong?"

Close. Too close. To her horror, Erin felt suddenly on the verge of tears. Praying that he hadn't noticed the wetness in her eyes, she pushed his hand away and turned her face down. "Neither my children nor my love life is any of your business," she snapped, shrugging off the sadness with sudden hostility.

"Wrong. It's Friday, remember? Time to renegotiate the terms of our agreement. That puts me right in the center of your potential love life." He moved behind the snowman and looked over his shoulder to get himself into her line of vision. "I look forward to renegotiations tonight."

"I look forward to driving your car," Erin retorted.

Nathan chuckled. "You are so good for my ego, Librarian."

Erin opened the door and threw off the snowsuit and the various accessories, then pulled on her coat and looked more or less like an adult again. She stomped through the snow to the black car, slightly whitened by the onslaught of snow.

"Well, let's go, hotshot," she called to Nathan, who had continued to sculpt the snowbaby while he waited for her. "I want to see how fast this thing goes."

She pretended not to notice Nathan's wince.

That evening, Erin slammed the door behind them as they got home, then apologized when Nathan jumped and looked at her with a question in his eyes. "Sorry, a draught."

It wasn't a draught.

Why did he have to be so darn charming? During their long dinner, she had all but forgotten the reasons she should keep her distance. She had been to that restaurant before, but it had never appeared so romantic to her. Yet she couldn't have described the decor, the music or even the food. Nathan had occupied all her attention with his stimulating conversation, warm glances and devastating smiles.

He didn't fight fair. She didn't even want to resist him. As it was, she would have difficulty not making advances herself.

The baby. Think about the baby.

"I had a great time tonight," Nathan said, linking their fingers together as they walked into the living room.

Erin pulled her hand away and sat down on the couch. Better get things official before anything happened. "So did I. But about the contract..."

"You want to renew it," he finished for her.

"Yes."

"Fine. Consider it renewed until next week."

Nathan watched with half-hearted amusement as she struggled—and failed utterly—not to show her mixture of disappointment and relief. He had gone all out tonight to charm her, using all the skills he possessed to show her he wasn't such a bad guy, to make her reconsider that ridiculous rule of hers not to get involved with an in-law. He was confident enough to know when he succeeded in charming a woman, but he also knew better than to push her any more than he already did with his light-hearted teasing. Although he didn't really believe he would ever be the long-term type, the marrying kind, a one-night stand wouldn't do either. Not this time. He didn't know what would come of it, but he looked forward to finding out.

First he'd just have to break through her ridiculous idea that getting involved with him would spark off World War III.

He stood up and got them soft drinks from the kitchen, touching her hand as he passed her the glass and sat down beside her. His librarian, heightened color in her cheeks, turned resolutely towards him, obviously digging deep into her reserves of small talk.

"You told me about your trip to China before. Was that the last place you were before you came home?"

Nathan hesitated. His mood darkened and his face must have reflected his unwillingness to share those memories because she immediately withdrew. "I'm sorry, it's none of my business. I was just wondering about what you said about having shared a bed with fleas and dogs."

Nathan cleared his throat. "No, it's no secret. I wasn't in China, but still in Asia. Didn't you hear about the floods?"

Erin nodded.

"Well, I spent two weeks there, and then I was a week in the mountains, where avalanches had struck. Entire villages were buried in snow."

"Were you in danger?"

"No. I went there at the same time as the rescue teams. There were blizzards and unbelievable weather conditions, but there was little risk of more avalanches."

"Could you work under those conditions?"

"I can work under any conditions." He grinned at her. "After all, it's just taking snapshots and picking up babes, remember?"

Erin blushed. "I'm sorry. I didn't mean to put down your work when I said that."

"I know."

"How dangerous were those avalanches?"

"Extremely. They smashed houses to pieces."

"A lot of people must have died."

"Yes."

She touched his arm briefly. "You must have seen some terrible things."

Nathan shrugged. "It can be a terrible world. I was lucky to be a bystander, not a victim. And I was grateful that this time I could help with the rescue work. For two or three days after the avalanches struck, several people were found alive buried in the snow." He did not mention the frantic battle between hope and despair during those days and nights spent digging at the mountainside in the blinding blizzard, the lifeless bodies he had uncovered from the smothering snow.

There was no purpose in thinking about the baby girl he had dug up, frozen arms still wound tightly around a stuffed lion. No one needed to know the shock he'd felt as his thoughts strayed immediately to his little niece, whose face he had never seen.

"Do you specialize in natural disasters?"

He shook his head, dragging his thoughts back to the present, but her question sent them straight back to the past. "Not particularly. Natural disasters, man-made disasters... You could say I specialize in suffering." He forced a self-deprecating smile and shrugged. "The empty faces of torture victims, the glazed eyes of starving infants, the dry eyes of the sole survivors, that's my work."

Erin's big eyes were looking at him with compassion. "That must be difficult."

Nathan shrugged, pushing her sympathy away. "To take snapshots? To hold up a camera and press a button? That's easy. Living through war and famine, having everything taken away from you, that's difficult. Watching the murder of your family, living through rape or torture, that's difficult."

He grabbed his glass and emptied it in one big gulp before slamming it back on the table and leaning back. He stared up at the ceiling while he spoke, almost unaware of the words forming on his tongue.

"All I do is make money from their suffering, then fly off to Spain for a holiday when I tire of watching babies starve to death."

"Nathan..." Her hand was on his shoulder now, gently kneading the tense muscles. "You help. You know you do so much more than the rest of us, who simply look at your pictures. You tell the world what is happening, how horrible it is. There is nothing more anyone expects you to do.''

Steeling himself, Nathan glanced up, preparing to push her away. He did not need this. Her compassion was making him weak. He needed strength, not weakness; strength to get over this burn-out, to reclaim the savage humor that made his work bearable and gave him the resilience to continue.

Tears sparkled in her eyes. Shaking his head ruefully, he reached out and stroked one from the corner of her eye. ''I hope you're crying for the right reasons, Librarian. Don't cry for me. Cry for the victims.''

She hiccuped, roughly brushing the tears away with the back of her hand. ''Did it ever occur to you that you may be a victim too?''

He didn't answer. He couldn't answer. Something had lodged in his throat, making speech impossible. His hands were curled into a fist, nails biting into the palms as his thoughts turned darker and darker. He didn't even notice it until Erin took one of his fists in her soft hands, pulling the curled fingers open with an effort. A tear fell from her cheek and into his palm, warm and wet. Gently she rubbed the dampness into his skin, then closed his fingers over it. "Don't be so angry with yourself, Nathan. You care."

Nathan jerked his head up, violently swallowing the lump in his throat. "What would you know about that, Librarian? I'm the bastard who mistreats your sister-in-law, remember? Who didn't attend his father's funeral or his sister's wedding. All those things you hate me for."

Erin flinched.

"I don't hate you, Nathan. You're nothing like I thought you would be." She shrugged helplessly. "You must have had your reasons. I shouldn't be so quick to judge. You were right, I don't know the circumstances."

"I had no good reason, Erin." His voice was gritty. "It would perhaps have been a bit problematic, but if I had really wanted to I could have come home at any time. I didn't because I didn't feel like it. Because I didn't want to. Because I *don't* care. That's it."

Her fingers stroked his cheek once, then she stood up and after a small hesitation leaned forward and kissed him on the forehead. "Goodnight, Nathan. Thank you for today."

She was gone, leaving him only with the warm imprint of her kiss on his forehead. He rubbed at his skin and swallowed hard. How had that woman got under his skin with her soft voice and gentle questions? Never, ever before had he even come close to talking about the tragedies he had seen in terms other than professional. He never admitted, even to himself, how much it disturbed him. He ignored the nightmares, the bitter grief he felt for the loss of hope he was so used to seeing. Among his colleagues he was known for his brutal, sometimes grotesque sense of humor, and although he took great care in approaching people with respect and compassion he always kept his emotions locked away, in much the same manner as he refused to allow himself to have feelings towards his family. Such as it was. Such as it ever had been.

He leaned forward, resting his head on his hands, and stared into the carpet, seeing only painful memories. All those years, and he had never allowed himself to think about his parents' rejection, never allowed himself to feel the pain of it.

He gritted his teeth. He was certainly feeling the full effect of it now. So many years later, and the pain re-emerged as if it had never left. Mother was gone, Father was gone, and he hadn't asked them why he could never be the son they wanted. As a boy he had wondered, he'd been confused, then hurt and angry. He hadn't understood why they couldn't love him, and he'd never asked. Instead, he had locked himself away from those feelings, displaying a polite, friendly but distant face to the world.

Why was this coming back to haunt him now? He suspected it had something to do with the red-haired librarian who kept interrupting his thoughts and messing with his dreams. He might convince himself he merely wanted her, that he enjoyed her company, enjoyed watching her fight the attraction between them, and knowing he would eventually win her over— but it wasn't true. He wanted the same thing from her as he had longed for from his parents. Unconditional acceptance. Love.

He drew in a sharp breath as the thought slammed into him. God, he needed something stronger than a soft drink. A sledgehammer came to mind. Something, anything to drown these types of thoughts.

Where had that word come from? Never before had he connected that word with a feeling, or with a woman.

Love. As if exploring a tooth cavity with his tongue, he tested the word, pushed it around in his mind.

Could that be happening to him? So fast? A few laughs, tumbles in the snow, the touch of a hand to his shoulder? A handful of stolen kisses, a hesitant smile in her eyes, and suddenly his heart had been stolen by a shy, red-haired librarian? Was he falling in love?

Love. He had never trusted that fraught word since the first time his mother looked at him with that distant look. That quizzical, slightly puzzled look, as if she had just noticed him and was wondering what he was doing there.

With a violent shudder he repressed the image, sending it back where it belonged, and stood up, closing his mind off to emotions and memories. His steps were soft on the stairs, and although he gazed with longing in the direction of Erin's room he did not pause on the way to his own bed.

The twins stayed over that weekend, keeping Erin busy, and during the following week she didn't see much of Nathan. They frequently met over coffee in the morning, and their conversation was friendly enough, but impersonal.

He almost seemed to be avoiding her. She tried to keep in mind that he was adhering to the terms of their contract and reminded herself that she wanted them to keep to that contract. They were to have the relationship of a brother and sister, that was it.

Nevertheless, she couldn't help but feel just a little bit rejected.

She could sense that his revelations that evening had been more than he had been prepared to give, but she was nevertheless pleased he had confided in her. Obviously he had his demons to battle with beneath that carefree surface. There were shadows behind the laughing eyes, even if they were buried deep under humor and that devil-may-care attitude.

Then it was Friday again. At work, things dragged on. Happy as she was with her job, there were times when she wished she could be doing something else. Her most secret wish was to be writing books instead of cataloging them. Ever since her Masters thesis, her dream had been to make a living writing anthropological books or articles. Perhaps some day she could make that dream come true.

In the meantime, this was second best. But right now she wished she was somewhere else. She'd spent the whole morning battling with her computer, which was in a particularly foul mood. The two adversaries were intently growling at one another when they were interrupted shortly before noon.

''Miss Avery!'' Without looking, she knew that Mrs Appleton was sailing towards her at full speed with a client in tow. The only time she was called Miss Avery around here was when clients were referred to her.

''Great,'' she moaned under her breath. ''Just when I need half an hour more to finish this.''

Mrs Appleton came to a halt at her desk, beaming at her The Smile. Erin knew what that meant: ''Take a good look at this one, young woman, maybe he's your Mr Right!'' She was a hopeless romantic and an impossible matchmaker. The fact that none of the prospective Mr Rights had so far captured Erin's interest did not deter her.

She tried not to think of Mrs Appleton's likely response to her fatherless pregnancy.

"The gentleman needs some references to rituals and tribal customs. I informed him you were our expert on the subject."

Erin put on her professional smile and turned towards her client. "An expert may be an overstatement but I'll certainly try to assist..." Her voice faded when she got a look at the "gentleman."

Nathan grinned unabashed under her glare.

Erin recovered. "Er—why don't you have a seat, sir?"

Mrs Appleton bustled away.

"What are you doing here, Nathan?" she muttered to him as he lowered himself into the narrow chair next to her desk.

"You are an information specialist. I need some information."

"On rituals and tribal customs?" she asked with a straight face, trying to ignore how good he looked in his usual leather jacket and black jeans and the way his warm gaze melted her insides.

"Exactly."

She peered suspiciously at him. "Are you sure you are here for information?"

His eyes opened wide. "Why, Miss Avery, you don't think this was strictly a ploy to see you?"

She chewed her lip in sudden uncertainty.

He leaned across the desk and whispered, "Actually, it was. But if you don't tell the kind Mrs Appleton, I won't either."

She grinned in sudden relief, but Nathan's face turned serious once again and he pulled a notebook and a pen from his jacket pocket.

"However, I do need some information."

"Yes?"

"I'm researching courting rituals."

Erin blinked. "You're researching courting rituals?" she repeated.

He nodded innocently, his green eyes angelic as he gazed at her.

"Yes. It's Friday. Renegotiation day. I need to learn how one courts a red-haired librarian who plays in the snow and looks great in a towel."

Hiding a grin, Erin frowned in pretended concentration as she turned to her computer and tapped on the keyboard. "Hm, librarians…courting rituals… No, I'm afraid I come up empty, Mr Chase. Perhaps you ought to consider writing that book yourself?"

His laughter echoed around the small library, drawing an approving glance from Mrs Appleton at the circulation desk.

"I might just do that. Are you free for research after work?"

"What do you have in mind?"

His elbows on her cluttered desk, chin on knuckles, he leaned forward. "A roller coaster."

"A roller coaster," she repeated, dumbfounded. She already felt she was on a roller coaster whenever she was around him, but that could hardly be what he meant.

"Do you like them?"

"Roller coasters? Wild screaming and hysteria? What's there not to like? You do mean like in an amusement park?"

His eyes filled with laughter. "Do you have some other kind in mind?"

Fighting back the blush, she fiddled with her pen. "OK, you're taking me to the amusement park? In the midst of winter? Most of the snow may have melted, but it'll be back soon, you know."

"You love playing in the snow, so I thought the amusement park wouldn't be far off the mark."

The idea was tempting. She loved amusement parks and frequented them with her young brothers, but as an adult she had never been to one without a small, sticky hand in each of hers and a hundred things to worry about.

"I don't think amusement parks are even open this time of year, Nathan."

"Yep. This one is. A new shopping center is opening across the road from the park, and they're using this to draw in new customers. It'll be open today and over the weekend, unless it snows again. Pick you up at four?"

Ignoring her better judgement, Erin nodded. It couldn't hurt, she told herself once again. Last Friday had gone well. They had grown closer as friends, as the in-laws they needed to be. She could have fun with Nathan for the day; she'd just have to make sure that the contract was renewed at the end of the evening, as it had been last week.

There was no harm in spending time with him. She was just playing a tour guide and a friendly in-law, as Sally had asked her.

Right?

"Oh, my God!"

Erin laughed at Nathan's panicked utterance

as the roller coaster began climbing the first hill. She had managed to get them the first car. Now there was nothing but the cloudy sky ahead and gravity pulling at their backs.

For once, she had the upper hand, and was feeling quite smug about it. "I can't believe you've never been on one of these rides before! Didn't you have any fun as a kid?"

Nathan didn't look too good. "I still think we should have started with a smaller one," he said, his knuckles white on the steel bars. "Worked our way up. The one with the swans and angels looked nice."

"Chicken," she teased. It was hard to believe that this globe-trotting daredevil who thrived on danger was actually nervous about a simple roller-coaster ride. She grinned. Somehow, it made him all the more endearing.

He glared at her, dark brows drawn together in a threatening frown. "If that grin of yours gets any wider, Miss Librarian, you will be needing stitches."

She giggled. "Don't sulk, Nathan. Enjoy the view!"

"Oh, my God," he breathed again as their wagon at last crested the hill and paused, offering a breathtaking, but alarming, view of the road ahead. Weakening, Erin put aside her reserves about touching him and put her arms around him, hugging him as tightly as she could with the restraints in the way. "Don't worry. It's fun. Just hold on to me and scream."

"I'll remember you said that," Nathan muttered, before grabbing hold of her as they plummeted down into the abyss.

"My plan backfired," Nathan grumbled good-naturedly as they walked away from the ride, holding hands. "This did not go at all as planned. You were supposed to seek shelter in my protective arms, not the other way around."

Erin giggled. "The end result was the same, right?" She had enjoyed those exhilarating minutes, the secure prison of Nathan's arms even more exciting than the ride. She knew her hand did not belong where it was, enveloped by his warm grasp, but she was too weak to break the contact.

"Yeah, but at a gruesome blow to my masculinity." He looked at her, his brows heavy. "You realize that in order to protect my reputation I will have to silence you by any means necessary?''

''Mmm... I'm susceptible to bribes.'' Erin eyed an ice-cream stand. ''Three scoops, please.''

''Ice cream? In this weather? I'm surprised the stand is even open.''

Erin freed her hand to pull the scarf tighter around her neck and do up the top button on her coat. ''OK, I'm ready now. Yes, please. Chocolate, chocolate and chocolate.''

''Women and their chocolate,'' Nathan muttered, but he did get her a cone, and a tricolored one for himself. They strolled into a tent to keep warm and found a seat at a tiny table.

''What flavors did you get?'' she asked, devouring her chocolate ice cream.

''Guess.'' He held the cone out to her. She hesitated only a second, then her tongue flicked out at the top scoop, its color similar to Nathan's eyes. ''Mint.''

''And the others?''

The middle scoop was a pale yellow. ''Banana,'' she proclaimed after a brief taste. ''And the lowest one is chocolate. I'd recognize it anywhere even without tasting.'' She sampled it anyway. One should never forego chocolate.

He grinned, and continued eating his ice cream. ''I thought it would be prudent to co-ordinate our tastes, so I chose chocolate as the bottom scoop.''

She nearly choked on her chocolate cone.

''What do you mean, co-ordinate our tastes?'' she demanded.

Nathan's eyes were alight with that wicked glow she had come to recognize. ''Just in case. There is that contract to discuss. Some experimenting might be necessary to see if the premises have changed. We wouldn't want any irrelevant factors interfering with the validity of the conclusion.''

Erin swallowed as warmth crept up her face. He was grinning at her, the look in his eyes both teasing and challenging. Banana, mint and chocolate blended on her tongue, the cool taste suddenly so much more than a calorie indulgence.

They finished their ice creams in silence, then wandered around the park for a while before the cold forced them to escape to the car. It was getting dark anyway. Darkness came earlier and earlier these days.

During the drive home, she watched his strong hands on the wheel and an unbidden image had them somewhere else. She pictured those long, sensitive fingers as they had sculpted a face on her snowbaby, then her imagination had them gently touching her own face. Up the side of her neck, into her hair, tracing the curve of her ear...

She groaned.

Nathan glanced over at her. "Is something wrong?"

In the dusky interior of the car, Erin blushed.

"No, just something I was thinking about."

Enviously, she eyed Nathan's hands. That was one lucky wheel.

She suddenly realized he had been talking while she had been indulging in illicit fantasies about his hands. "I'm sorry, what did you say?"

"I asked if you'd mind eating at home tonight? I'll cook. It's pretty late, but I'll keep it simple."

"You cook? *And* do the dishes? My, why hasn't some woman enslaved you yet?"

He chuckled. "I guess I'm pretty wild. It would take a lot of work to domesticate me."

"I can imagine," she murmured. "They have an operation for that, you know. Worked fine for Erika's cat."

Nathan frowned for a moment, his eyes on the road ahead. Then he winced. "I hope you're not talking about what I think you are." He looked sideways at her. "Nah, you're too much of a lady to make a joke like that."

She was. At least, she had been. She closed her eyes in mortification. What had come over her to say a stupid thing like that?

"I'm sorry," she blurted out. "It was a silly, adolescent joke."

He laughed, a soft, rumbling sound that had her toes curling. "Don't apologize. Jokes are meant to be silly." He looked sideways at her, still smiling. "I'm hoping I'll get to see that smile on a regular basis too. You frown way too much, you know."

"Yep, neurotic mess, that's me," she muttered as the car rolled into the driveway and came to a stop. Nathan undid his seat belt, then leaned over and kissed her unexpectedly on the cheek.

"Neurotic is cute," he said with a wink.

CHAPTER FIVE

DINNER was simple, a pasta and ham dish baked in the oven, plus garlic bread and salad, but it was delicious nevertheless. Seeing Nathan wearing an apron was a definite bonus. She made a mental note not to tell Mrs Appleton at the library about Nathan's culinary skills. The good lady would immediately have them bound, cataloged and shelved in the couples department.

During dinner their conversation strayed to Christmas, reminding Erin that he had intended to stay until after the holiday.

''Where are you going next? Do you have an assignment lined up already?''

Nathan was still for a moment, then he shrugged. He stood up and began piling the dishes by the sink. ''I'm not sure I'm going far this time.'' He shrugged again, this time with a wry grin. ''I might just settle down and get a 'real job', like Dad always put it. That's why I've got involved in that advertising business.'' He ushered her into the living room.

147

"A real job?" Erin flung herself down on the couch, amused by his choice of words. "According to your sister, you're one of the top photographers in the world!"

Nathan chuckled. "As you are fond of telling me, my sister tends to exaggerate when it comes to Big Brother." He grabbed the remote control and turned on the television, switching channels until he reached a news program, but keeping the sound muted. Pictures of a stranded ship appeared on the screen. "I'm good at what I do, I know that. But things have changed. I'm getting tired, jaded. I think eventually it will begin to show in my work, so perhaps it is time to move on."

Erin was silent, waiting for him to continue. He switched the television off and threw the remote control on the coffee-table. Then he leaned forward, resting his elbows on his knees as he searched for words.

"I've always wanted to show the story, the lives, behind the faces. When we see a newspaper photograph of someone starving or injured, of refugees or disaster victims, most of us never realize it could just as well be us. They are people just like us, with homes, education, jobs, all of which were suddenly snatched away from them by war or famine.''

He shrugged helplessly.

''I was obsessed with my work.'' He chuckled derisively and gestured in her direction. ''Well, you know that. It was like some kind of terrible addiction, capturing each ruined life. As if capturing it on film could somehow change things.'' He paused. A vein was throbbing in his temple and his hands were clenched into fists. Erin felt her heart contract in sympathy as she was reminded of how painful this subject was for him. ''I guess I finally realized that nothing I do over there with my camera changes anything for those people. So...I quit.''

''You quit? What do you mean, you quit? You work freelance, don't you?''

''Not any more. Look, no camera!'' He pointed at his chest. ''It's been so long since I didn't have a camera around my neck every day that I feel like I was just let out of a noose.''

''I see.''

Erin was silent for a while, and slowly sipped her red wine. He was still distracted, staring at the dark television screen.

"So, what are you going to do with the rest of your life?" she asked at last.

Nathan gave a deep sigh as he leaned back and stared up at the ceiling with a frown. "Well, I'm looking into the advertising thing, but to tell you the truth I have no idea. I knew I wanted to be a photographer when I was a teenager. I'm having my first identity crisis now at the grand age of thirty-one."

"You can still be a photographer. There are other possibilities than war and disaster news. Who knows, advertising could be fun."

"Maybe." He shrugged. "Of course there are all sorts of possibilities. But fashion models and shampoo bottles are just not what I'm used to seeing through my lens."

His eyes narrowed on her as he tossed his head in a familiar manner. She had come to recognize that movement for what it was, a bodily expression of a lid being shut on his private thoughts. "Enough about me. What about you? Did you always want to be a librarian?"

"No," she admitted. "Don't get me wrong, I love my job. But it wasn't my first choice."

He waited for her to elaborate.

"You know I studied anthropology. I wanted to do research in the field, but my allergies prevent me from doing any work where there is a possibility of animals or even plants being around. And allergic anthropologists aren't exactly in demand." She smiled self-deprecatingly. "So I specialized in city behavior, the modern behavior of *Homo sapiens*. But jobs in that sector are hard to come by."

"What do you mean by modern behavior?"

"You know, body language, behavior in a group, city eccentricities and such things."

"So you're a specialist in body language?"

Erin flushed at the teasing note in his voice. With all her expertise, she had never been able to control her own body language, and Nathan seemed unselfconscious about the messages he sent out.

"You seem to know a thing or two about that yourself," she muttered.

Nathan nodded. "Yes. That's one of the things you learn when you watch the world through the lens of a camera. Have you thought about teaching?"

She shook her head. "That's not for me. I'm just not teacher material. I took the degree in library studies, and most of the time I'm really quite happy with working at the library. I've always loved books.'' A soft sigh escaped her lips. ''Although I can't deny that occasionally I long for more challenging work. Something where I could make good use of my anthropology degree. Perhaps write articles or small anthropological pieces.'' She shrugged philosophically. ''Perhaps some day.''

Nathan put an arm around her shoulders, squeezing briefly. ''Well, welcome to the thirty-something identity-crisis club.''

''Hey! I'm only twenty-seven!'' she protested, poking him with her elbow. ''Thirty is so many light-years away that I'm not even in that galaxy yet!''

''Don't worry, you'll get there eventually.'' He grinned. ''Meanwhile, I will grant you an honorary membership, based on that cute little wrinkle between your eyes.''

''What wrinkle?''

''The one that is most certainly going to appear if you keep frowning at me every time I kiss you.''

''What?'' Erin pulled slightly back as he moved closer.

''See? You're frowning. I tell you: it happens every time.''

"Maybe you should take a hint, then, and stop kissing me."

He shook his head slowly, a smile hovering on his lips. "I'm sorry, but I can't do that."

"Why not?"

"It's the only way to remove that frown."

"But…"

Before she could point out the obvious flaw in his logic, she was being kissed. Completely, as if he had been starving for her. Immersed in his scent, his warmth, she was lost until he broke the kiss and added a fleeting one on her nose.

She gave a big sigh and rested her head on his chest, the simmering desire inside giving way to the sleepy fog that always followed her alcohol intake.

"Something wrong?"

"No. That was a nice kiss."

The rumble of his laughter tickled her ear.

"If my kisses are *nice*, perhaps I need to re-evaluate my strategy."

"You know what I mean." She shrugged and buried her face in his shirt, inhaling his scent, then rubbed her nose affectionately against him. "I'm not the most eloquent person in the world," she mumbled. "How would you like me to describe them, anyway?"

"Hot?" he suggested. "Searing? Scorching? Blazing? Sizzling?"

Reluctantly lifting her head away from his strong and steady heartbeat, Erin grabbed a cushion and whacked the grinning thesaurus. She giggled. That last glass of wine had probably been over the top. She had no tolerance for alcohol and was feeling more and more light-headed by the minute. "You're fun, Nathan. It's fun to be with you."

"Thank you. Same to you."

Erin stared at his smiling lips for long moments, debating whether to risk another kiss. Then her attention was drawn to the tiny creases in his cheeks and she lifted her hand and traced them with a finger. "And you're cute too."

"*Cute?*" He swore softly. "Just the compliment every man wants to hear. Are you tipsy, Librarian?"

She nodded solemnly. "I must be. I wouldn't be telling you that you're cute if I were fully sober."

"I see," Nathan murmured, laughter bubbling in his voice. "Anything else you'd like to share while your condition allows?"

She peered suspiciously at him. "Are you taking advantage of me?"

"Do you want me to?"

Erin digested his question and came up with a resounding yes, only seconds later to be followed by a somewhat reluctant no.

She was leading him on. Better back-paddle quickly.

"I think we should postpone renegotiations," she confessed. "I can't be trusted at the moment. I might agree to spend the night being ravished by you."

"And you don't think that would be a good idea?" His voice was indulgent, almost as if he were talking to a child.

"No. You see..." She leaned towards him and whispered, "I have this secret. It's sort of a big secret and even if it wouldn't mess with our family I couldn't have a fling with you."

"Are you going to tell me your secret?"

"No," she answered regretfully. "No one can know. I'm sorry." Her mouth opened in a huge yawn. "I'm really sleepy."

Nathan kissed her on the forehead, then stood up and pulled her to her feet. "Go to bed, Librarian. Hurry, before you agree to being ravished."

"Right. You know," she added, pausing by the door, "you're too nice. It would be much easier to resist you if you weren't so nice."

"Perhaps pretending to be nice is just a part of my nefarious scheme."

Erin only smiled and then sent him a finger kiss before shuffling to her room.

Had she really told him last night that he was cute and that she had a big secret and that she was tempted to be ravished by him? Erin blinked, her head sideways on the pillow as she stared at the alarm clock. It had woken her up at the usual time even though it was her Saturday off. Memories of last night had then yanked her to full consciousness.

She should have known better than to drink that third glass of red wine. But it could have been worse. At least she hadn't told him the details of her secret. He didn't know that she was going to have a baby.

She threw the covers aside and put her robe on, and knotted the belt with harsh movements, all thoughts of sleep gone. The way she kept forgetting her goals was almost frightening. Never before had she had any trouble with her plans; been tempted to throw away her safe and calm existence, to forget all the reasons why she wanted a life alone.

And just when she was about to put those plans into action, Nathan had come along and messed with both her mind and her heart until her head was spinning.

Leaving her room, she could hear the shower running. The door to Nathan's room was open, and she caught a glimpse of his unmade bed. She ignored those rumpled sheets and walked down the stairs with her eyes closed, holding on to the banister for support. Squeezing her eyes shut did not do much to keep the images away though. Pictures played ruthlessly behind her closed lids. Images of that naked back she'd only seen once, and then bathed in moonlight. At this very moment, the warm spray from the shower was pounding on his skin, running in rivulets down his body, caressing every square inch just as her wayward fingers were itching to.

Theoretically she could sneak in the bathroom, into the shower, still in her nightgown and come up behind him. She could put her hands on his shoulders and bend her head to his warm, wet back, imprinting the broad area with her lips. It would take some time, but she was a thorough and conscientious person and would take all the time needed for the task.

Dreamily she slid down on a chair in the kitchen, forgetting even to start the coffee brewing. Of course, the subject would have to co-operate. He would have to stand still and wait until she had finished doing justice to the whole area. It wouldn't do, for example, for him to turn around when she was only halfway done, and melt her insides with a combination of flaming green gaze and a knowing, blazing smile. It would be out of the question for him to grab the showerhead and slowly run it over her body, soaking her nightgown with the warm water until it left nothing to the imagination. It would definitely be a bad idea if he were to grab a bar of soap and kneel down to wash her feet, pushing the wet cotton out of the way as he worked his way up her legs. And of course it was absolutely unthinkable for him to grab the drenched material and yank it over her head and out of the way before crushing their wet bodies together and giving her the *nicest* kiss ever…

"Good morning, Librarian. Hungover?"

Oh, God! Jumping to her feet, Erin busied herself with the coffee-grinder, her face burning. She couldn't look at him now—he'd instantly know what she'd been thinking about. Heck, one look into her eyes and he'd have the details right down to the brand of soap.

With trembling hands she made the coffee and tried to calm down. It was a while until she trusted herself to face him, and when she did he was frowning. Probably wondering why she had jumped away from the table and ignored him and his question.

"No. No hangover, but I'm still half-asleep," she said, finally daring to meet his eyes, but quickly looking away again. He was just too beautiful. The image sent a delectable shiver down her spine. His hair was still wet from the shower, loosely combed back from his face, but falling forwards again. Replace that concerned frown with a wicked grin combined with a steamy look of passion, and he'd look just as he had in her fantasy.

Well, except that he had clothes on. He was wearing black, as he usually did. Jeans and a thick knitted turtleneck sweater, the sleeves rolled up. He looked absolutely scrumptious. Who needed breakfast with that feast at the kitchen table? She'd cuddle close in his lap and bury her hands in his hair, then begin by nibbling on his ears and neck...

No, no, no, no! No more fantasies!

Nathan coughed and her eyes snapped open as she realized that she had been standing there with eyes squeezed shut and palms pressed against her ears in an attempt to power down her overheated imagination.

"Are you OK, sweetheart?"

His grin told her he might be guessing all too accurately at the reason for her strange behavior.

"Yes, yes, I'm fine." She grabbed a cup and poured some of the brewing coffee, then gulped down the scalding liquid, ignoring how it burnt her mouth. Caffeine, and lots of it. It was her only salvation now, a roadmap out of that fantasy-world.

"I never really become drunk enough to get a hangover," she blabbered, stalling while she waited for the caffeine to kick in. "I get a bit light-headed and silly, as you saw last night, and then I just get sleepy and drop off."

He chuckled. "I don't mind silly," he said, grinning at her. Erin blushed, trying not to think about the stupid things she had said, but not succeeding terribly well. Was he at all wondering about her "secret"?

"I've been thinking about what you said last night."

Uh-oh. It seemed he was.

"You have?" she croaked.

"Yes. I think I may have a business proposal for you."

She blinked, gathering her thoughts. "A business proposal?" she repeated. How could her secret be linked to a business proposal?

"I think we should do a book together."

"A *book*?" She promised herself not to repeat the next thing he said, but what *was* he talking about?

"Yes." He put his elbows on the table and leaned towards her. "It struck me when you talked about your anthropological interest in group behavior and city life, and your interest in writing about that. It would make a great book. My photographs, your anthropological expertise."

He described his project animatedly, giving her time to regroup and focus on his words.

He had an idea about a book combining photographs of people in the city with anthropological passages about their behavior, the messages and signals they sent out.

"Well, what do you think?"

He was looking at her expectantly.

"I… It sounds interesting," she hedged.

He chuckled. "Ever cautious."

She was more than intrigued. It sounded like
a wonderful way to kick-start a new career.
But what was he thinking? Was he planning to
stick around? How long did it take, anyway,
to create such a book? Would they be working
together, or each on their own part?

She had a thousand questions, but inborn
caution held them back while she picked and
chose the most innocent ones.

"How… What do you have in mind? Do
you provide the pictures and I write the text?
Or do you want me to write the text and then
you try to create pictures that fit?"

"I was thinking more along the lines of this
being a team effort. We could make some
plans for what kind of things we are looking
for, then we would go out together and scout
for subjects. Then we could write the text together."

Together. He wanted them to go through every step in this process together.

Erin clenched her fists, torn between exhilaration and panic. She felt like running straight out to start off the project, but she knew it would only complicate things between her and Nathan.

Unless they could have a simple, platonic working relationship. Another contract? This one without heady Friday kisses and renegotiations?

Wishful thinking. Except that the thought was accompanied by regret, not hope.

She was so confused.

"But aren't you leaving soon? This will take a lot of time."

He shrugged. "I don't know if I'm leaving. I'm considering settling down here. Buying a house. As you said, my only family is here."

Erin's heart jumped into her throat and lodged there, making her unable to speak for a while.

"You're staying in Maine?" she croaked at last. "For good?"

All her plans had hinged on his leaving. She had made this deal with herself, to allow herself a few weeks with him before having her baby and settling down for the rest of her life. If he wasn't leaving, everything could turn complicated.

And yet, why had there been that split-second thrill of happiness when he first mentioned staying?

"Perhaps. Nothing is definite yet." He studied what she belatedly realized must be a look of abject panic painted all over her face. She schooled her features into what she hoped was a passable smile.

"Sally would be thrilled."

"You don't look thrilled yourself."

"I'm not… My opinion doesn't matter."

"It does to me. Why don't you want me to stay, Librarian?"

"It's none of my business where you stay," she hissed. He did not play by the rules. Why did he keep confronting her? Every little thing she wanted to keep secret seemed to be an open book to him.

"You're afraid, Librarian. The idea of me sticking around scares the hell out of you, because of your silly ideas about in-law terrorism."

"I'm not afraid of anything," she bristled, annoyed at the challenge in his eyes, the intensity of his features as he leaned towards her. It was a look she knew and had come to associate with his maddening mind-reading tricks.

He leaned back, the seriousness replaced with a bland smile. ''Good. Then there is nothing to stop you from collaborating with me on this book, is there?''

She was trapped. Although she knew that for her peace of mind the smartest thing to do was to turn down this assignment, she couldn't make herself do so. Such an assignment was a dream come true for her, and he had to know that. If she wanted to do a similar work on her own, it would be close to impossible to find a publisher. Working with a photographer of Nathan's caliber and reputation, that part would be a breeze.

''No,'' she conceded, for the moment pushing aside her turbulent emotions and allowing her enthusiasm to show. ''It *is* a terrific idea, Nathan. I'd love to give it a try.'' Ideas were already swirling through her mind now that her mind was made up. Man-woman relationships at different ages; children interacting together; children and adults; friends, strangers and lovers. Locations—a busy street, a shopping mall, bars... The possibilities were endless.

Chuckling at the light in her eyes, Nathan reached for a notepad and a pen from the top of the fridge and pushed them towards her. She grabbed them and began jotting down ideas, for once unaware of his scrutiny. Her plan to end their budding relationship when their siblings returned was fairly obvious to him. This idea had been a marvellous way to keep them together—and it was a great career move for both of them.

Rarely had he seen her so excited. Words were spilling from her mouth as well as from her pen to the paper, and he was soon caught up in her enthusiasm.

''Why don't we go right now and see what we come across?'' he suggested, receiving a brilliant smile in return.

The weekend passed quickly as they walked around Portland, developing their concepts and taking pictures, talking and planning.

Sunday evening found them standing over the dining-room table, where dozens of pictures displayed their scenes. Scrawled passages from Erin's notebook fitted each photograph.

"I don't know if the bathroom will ever be the same again, but it's great that you could turn it into a darkroom. I was so impatient to see the pictures."

He chuckled. "Me too. The bathroom is a luxury compared to the primitive conditions I've worked under. And it's not in that bad a shape, is it?"

"Mmm. I'm sure Thomas and Sally will find the red light bulb a nice, romantic addition to their bathroom. Not to mention the trays in the bathtub."

"This was a terrific weekend, Erin. I think we're doing great here."

Something in his tone made her look up from the table and at his face, meeting a smoldering fire in the depths of his eyes. One step brought him to her side.

"Come here, Librarian."

One minute they were standing, the next minute he was on the living-room couch and had pulled her with him so she was kneeling across his lap. It reminded her deliciously of their first kiss. Was there a follow-up session scheduled? After their closeness over the weekend, the idea was so tempting that she couldn't help herself. She relaxed against him, her hands on his shoulders as she gazed into the smile in those green eyes.

''Do you still think I'm cute?'' he asked, fluttering his eyelashes at her and managing to look adorable instead of silly.

Despite her best efforts, she melted. ''Yeah. You're still cute.''

''Cute enough to kiss?''

''It's not Friday,'' she hedged, more to remind herself than to remind him. She told herself to stand up, but not a single muscle in her body was on her side. They were all on strike.

She didn't mind too much. His forearms rested across her thighs, practically burning holes in the denim. One of her hands stole down, trailed down his upper arm, over the bunched material of his sweater at his elbow, to the warm skin of his bare forearm.

''I know.'' He shifted his arm slightly to give her better access, and her fingers ran to the underside of his arm, exploring the bones where arm joined hand. ''We never got to the renegotiation bit. You didn't feel up to it.''

Erin blushed, her exploring fingers stopping on his wrist as she remembered her earnest explanation of why renegotiations would have to be postponed.

"We did, however, get to the experimenting part. Remember?"

She nodded, focusing on the knitted pattern around his shoulder.

That was a mistake. As he shifted the muscles of his upper arms moved, sparking off a chain reaction in her insides. She moved her gaze to his neck, then his ear, and then abandoned that whole thing and instead stared over his shoulder at the wall behind him. Her fingers were still around his wrist, and all of a sudden she could sense his pulse. Strong and steady, it answered to something primal inside her, tugging at longings and dreams she had never known were there.

Could two hearts really beat as one?

She swallowed and reminded herself that she would never find out.

"You said my kiss was *nice*, right? A mediocre grade if I ever heard one."

She dared a look at his face, knowing she'd find that grin there. Predictably, it lightened her own mood, pulled her out of the gloom that for a second had threatened to envelop her. Humor. It's the only way to survive in this world, he had said.

"Well, it was! Not mediocre, but very nice, I mean," she added, allowing a teasing smile to pull at her mouth. "There's nothing wrong with nice. Your kiss was perfectly adequate."

"Mmm." Nathan's eyes narrowed at her choice of adjective. "Adequate, eh? Well, I've been working on improving my technique."

"Really?"

"Yeah. I was hoping you'd take a test run and give me some feedback."

"Nathan?"

"Yes?"

"Why do our discussions always end with me in your lap?"

He threw his head back and laughed, then slid further down in the couch and pulled her down with him. "Because I like having you there. Plus, it's easier to catch you changing the subject on me. What do you say, Librarian? Will you assist me in perfecting my methodology?"

"You're impossible," she said wretchedly, even as she lowered her mouth to his, her errant fingers already caressing his face and finding their way into the warm softness of his hair. She pulled back an inch just before their lips met, and spoke against his mouth. "But… I'm not…grading you…again."

"Got it." His voice was barely a whisper. "No grades. Just practice." His hands encircled her waist, then stroked them up her back as he nipped at her lower lip, before soothing it with his tongue. "Lots and lots of practice."

"Flight 1532 from Athens, 6:30, December 2nd."

Erin stared down into her leather-bound diary. Only two days until Thomas and Sally were back.

Although the days at the library took forever to pass, the week had vanished in a haze. Nathan usually picked her up, charming Mrs Appleton's socks off every time. Erin didn't correct her assumptions, allowing her to be ecstatic over having brought the two of them together.

Anyway, she thought wryly, perhaps her assumptions weren't that far off the mark. They had spent almost every waking moment together the past few days. The afternoons were spent touring the city, spotting subjects for the camera, writing bits and pieces on various subjects.

And the evenings. Oh, lord, the evenings.

Nathan was getting lots and lots of practice.

And she was opening herself up for lots and lots of heartbreak.

Erin groaned and dropped her head down on her desk. What was she doing to herself? Every time it was harder to pull out of his arms, to go alone to her room to toss and turn, knowing he was right across the hall. And every time the feelings of guilt and remorse were stronger; yet she couldn't bring herself to get their relationship back on a chaste in-laws track. All her logical thoughts melted into a puddle of incoherent giddiness when that man was near. Her emotions were in such a jumble that she didn't even know where to begin at unraveling them. All she managed to do was to curse her weakness and strengthen her resolve, only to have it dissolve at her feet at one glimpse of that special smile in those emerald eyes.

Erin grabbed the telephone book off the desk and buried her head under it for good measure. Worst of all, she kept forgetting all the reasons she should keep him at a distance. Her family. Her baby. The appointment at the insemination clinic seven short weeks from now.

What would Nathan say when he found out she was expecting a baby? More than anyone, he would know there was no man in her life. Would he buy her vague story about a whirlwind romance and a man who'd left her alone and pregnant? Would he be suspicious? She winced at her own stupidity. Of course he would.

Two more days, and Thomas and Sally would be back. She'd move out, away from Nathan, away from the magical spell he had woven around her.

But there was still that book to work on.

She groaned aloud, remembering that with the book she had committed to a continuing relationship with Nathan. Without it, she could have walked out of his life in just a few days.

Her heart pounded harder as she began to realize the complex web she was weaving around herself. She would be conceiving her child in only a few weeks. By this weekend, she'd have to make sure things between her and Nathan would be strictly professional. She would have to do that in a way that Nathan would understand, so that he would co-operate in keeping their relationship—such as it was—away from their family.

She shuddered to think of the catastrophic consequences if Thomas or Sally got a whiff of what they'd been up to. They would instantly assume that the baby was Nathan's. She might even have to go through DNA screening before they would believe otherwise. Such complications could devastate their family, even split Sally and Thomas up into separate factions, each taking their sibling's side.

Stop overreacting and assuming the worst, Erin, she told herself as she felt sweat bead her forehead. She was panicking for no good reason. Nathan was a reasonable man. They'd had fun for a few weeks, and she had never led him to believe there would be more. On the contrary, she had again and again told him that even if she was kissing him, going out with him, laughing with him, there could be nothing between them.

She'd pick Thomas and Sally and her little niece up at the airport on Saturday morning. She'd get Nathan to come along with her and tell him on the way. That way he wouldn't have time to make a scene. They'd drive back with their siblings and little Natalie; she'd move out, and it would be over.

Except for the book.

She whimpered.

CHAPTER SIX

THIS was their last day together.

Erin glanced at the clock, hoping Nathan would get up soon. She wanted to see him before she left for work. This would be their last evening together and she wanted it to be special. She had made up her mind to postpone all her worries until tomorrow morning. Selfish, perhaps, but irresistible.

A slight sound drew her attention towards the stairs, visible through the open kitchen door. Her breath caught at the sight of him. He was on his way down, yawning, wearing pristine black pyjamas. Still creased, they were obviously fresh from a package. Instead of his usual gorgeous, he looked sweet, Erin thought, a bitter-sweet smile on her lips. Boyish, even, with his hair standing on end. Her heart somersaulted in her chest as he noticed her and sent her one of those lazy, devastating smiles.

''Good morning.'' Erin tried to hide her grin behind her coffee-cup, but he noticed and grinned right back before taking his place at the table.

"Like my pyjamas? I bought these just for you. I seem to recall that you didn't much care for my choice of nightwear when we first met."

Erin briefly fought back the blush, but then allowed it to spread over her face along with her smile. "Oh, I won't complain. Nothing looked good on you too," she said, marveling at her sudden boldness and getting her reward when he leaned over and kissed her quick and hard on the lips.

"Admit it, you just put those on," she accused. "They don't look slept in."

He just grinned and reached for the cereal, leaving her heart flip-flopping in her stomach.

Did he realize this was their last day together? Would he understand?

Suddenly she felt very nervous.

"I'm picking Thomas and Sally up at the airport early tomorrow morning," she told him, struggling to keep her voice calm and nonchalant. "Would you like to come?"

"Sure. Will you wake me up?"

"No problem. Five-thirty."

"Or I could wake you up."

The tone was unmistakable. She ignored him.

"Or we could wake each other up."

Knife in butter, butter on toast.

"Or, best of all, we could just skip the waking up bit altogether and not go to sleep at all."

Erin silenced him by stuffing a piece of buttered toast into his open mouth just as he was about to offer a new suggestion. It had been tempting to silence him in another way, to lean over and grab the silly-looking lapels on his pyjamas, pull him close and kiss him hard.

But why resist anyway?

She watched him finish the toast and drink from a small glass of orange juice, a frown on his forehead as something on the radio news distracted him from putting tantalizing images into her head.

The last Friday. What the hell.

Half a second later, she was in his lap. Behind her back, there was a clatter as he dropped his glass to the table. She cradled his face in her hands and kissed him deeply, desperately. They could have tonight, but after tomorrow there would be no more morning kisses. He tasted of orange juice and he hadn't shaved yet, the bristles feeling strange yet good against her skin.

"Mmm. I think I could develop a taste for aggressive women," Nathan murmured, wrapping his arms around her waist and pulling her even closer. His body heat penetrated easily through his cotton pyjamas, bringing images of a warm, inviting bed to her mind. "What's this for? Does it have anything to do with who wakes up whom tomorrow?"

He rubbed his nose against hers and gazed into her eyes with those probing eyes. She felt as if he was looking directly into her soul and shut her eyes against the invasion.

"Nathan..."

"Yes, sweetheart?"

She sat silently in his lap for a while, searching for words while her fingers gently moved over his face and memorized it. Would he understand? Did he know that there couldn't be anything more now that her brother and his sister were returning?

Desire was glittering in his eyes, mirroring that in her own, the sweetness of his mouth still lingering in hers. She would have the afternoon and this evening to luxuriate in his touch, his kisses. In holding hands and laughing. She would have the thrill of his regular, yet sudden and unexpected, tight hugs during their stroll through the city.

Could she have the night as well? Could she take what he offered, make love with him once before breaking it off? She had already broken all her own rules—how much more damage would it do to spend one night with him?

She wanted to. She wanted one night with this man. Why not? The answer was right there in front of her. They had already gone this far: there was no reason not to take what he had been offering all along, one night of emotional and physical fulfilment, a completeness at last. Although she had never allowed the word love to enter her thoughts, she knew she cared deeply for him, that her feelings ran much deeper than physical attraction. She wasn't sure how he felt, but at the moment it seemed enough and yet not too much.

In the background, the radio announced the time, jolting her back to reality. ''I have to go,'' she said, suddenly realizing how late she was. He didn't let her out of his arms, but lifted her up, kissing her all the way to the front door before allowing her feet to touch the floor again. He didn't release her right away, but held her against the warmth of his body for a long while before stepping back. His smile was bitter-sweet to her despairing eyes.

How can I tell him? How can I leave him?

She postponed the thought. Tomorrow morning. She would tell him tomorrow morning.

Tearing her gaze from him, she threw on her coat. Vaguely remembering the cold-weather forecast, she fished the worn leather gloves out of the pockets. Something fell to the floor and Nathan reached down to pick it up. He glanced at it casually and began handing it to her, then did a double take.

"What is this?"

Horrified, she saw that Nathan was holding the pamphlet she had picked up at the clinic all those weeks ago and then stuffed in a pocket and forgotten. She grabbed it from him and crammed it into her bag between layers of books, while searching furiously for a possible explanation. Too late, she realized her reaction had given her away. There was not just a single conclusion he could draw from finding this brochure in her belongings. For all he knew it could be a piece of junk mail.

She tried to shrug it off. "Nothing. Just a pamphlet I picked up somewhere. You know. Something to read in the dentist's waiting-room."

Nathan's eyebrows were drawn together in a frown. "Don't lie to me. You're practically radiating guilt. Is this your big secret, Erin? You are going to have a baby by a sperm donor?"

"Don't be ridiculous," she said, trying to laugh it off. "Of course not. I told you, it's just a piece of junk mail I picked up somewhere."

"You're a lousy liar, Erin." Nathan reached into her open bag and yanked the pamphlet back out. His jaw was clenched as he held it out of her reach. "'New Life Clinic,'" he read aloud. "'Sperm donation: have the baby you never thought you would have.'"

"Give me that!" The paper ripped as she grabbed the pamphlet from him for the second time. "It's none of your business."

"I'm making it my business! I can't believe this, Erin! I can't believe that you are actually going to have a child by some anonymous father!"

"He is not that anonymous," she snapped, ignoring for the moment that there were five possible fathers. "I know his statistics, down to his shoe size and his IQ. He will provide fine genes for my baby."

"He will provide fine genes for your baby?"

She'd thought her words sounded so sophisticated, but when they were reflected back at her in that deep, disbelieving baritone they sounded plain stupid.

Nathan was staring at her as if she'd gone completely mad.

"When is this supposed to happen?" He looked her over. "You're not pregnant now, are you?"

The horror in his eyes was all too visible.

"That's none of your business."

"I need to know, Erin. Tell me. Are you pregnant already?"

Before her unwillingness to answer could stop her, she had shaken her head in denial.

Nathan drew a deep breath. "OK. When did you plan to do this?"

"Soon."

"What does your family say about this?"

"They don't know," she muttered. "They won't ever find out. I will tell them the father is out of the picture."

Silence. She looked up. "You wouldn't tell them, would you?" she asked, uneasy about the unreadable look on his face.

Nathan ignored her question.

"What if you meet someone later on, fall in love, and want to have his baby? What happens to this child then?"

"What do you mean? Nothing will happen to it!"

"Really? You don't think there is any danger of you loving him or her less than the child that you make together with your lover? A child made from a combination of your genes and the genes of someone you love?"

"Of course not," she said in outrage. "A child is a child. You don't just throw the old one away when a new one comes along!"

Nathan's features looked as if they were carved in granite. "You'd be surprised at human nature when it comes to their offspring," he growled. "You shouldn't do this, Erin. You really shouldn't do this."

"I'll be thirty soon," Erin said in a low voice. "I don't want to wait too long to have

children.'' Not that time would make a difference, but he didn't need to know that.

''You're only twenty-seven. It seems a bit
soon to have given up hope already of finding
someone to father your children.''

She turned away from him and knelt down
to lace her shoes. ''I don't know why I'm discussing this with you, anyway. It's none of
your business who fathers my children.''

Nathan drew in a sharp breath. Erin jumped
as he slammed his fist against the wooden
door. ''Isn't it? What about us, Erin? Did you
ever consider how I would feel about this?
Were you ever going to tell me?''

She fumbled with her laces, tears clouding
her vision. She tried to answer, but her voice
wouldn't obey. Giving up on the laces, she
stood up and leaned against the door, feeling
exhausted.

Nathan shook his head in a violent move
and scowled at her. Never before had she seen
such coldness in his eyes.

''You weren't, were you? You were never
serious about us. About me. You never meant
our relationship to go anywhere.''

''Come on, Nathan.'' Her voice was weak,
and she straightened, trying to get a grip of

herself. "It's not like you were ever serious yourself. And I told you there couldn't be anything between us. You make it sound like I was just using you."

"Weren't you? Weren't you just having fun, a fling, before you settled down with your fatherless baby?"

"No," she cried. "I was…"

She wrapped her arms around herself, suddenly cold.

"I told you it couldn't happen. And we're not even lovers, Nathan. There was no *fling*. There is no *us*." Gazes clashed and held. She made one last desperate attempt to convince him. "It's not as if you're in love with me. Are you?"

Silence.

"I don't know." He shifted his weight awkwardly, the anger less visible, but still simmering near the surface. "I might be."

"You *might* be?" She thought she emitted a laugh, but it sounded like a sob. "Not exactly the three little words every woman longs to hear, are they?"

"Do you long for me to say them to you, Erin?"

Good question, but one she wasn't even going to think about. Romantic love had no place in her life. She stared at him, trying to read his thoughts instead of delving into her own. His voice held fiercely controlled emotion. Anger? Disappointment? Bruised pride? She couldn't tell. His eyes were shuttered even as his gaze probed hers, searching for an answer she couldn't give him. Her baby had to come first. She couldn't afford to fall in love, least of all with Sally's brother. Sally's brother, who for some reason was a stranger even to his own flesh and blood.

She would never allow herself to fall in love, and especially not with such a man, a man who under the smooth surface perhaps did not know how to love. He'd said himself that was the reason he stayed away, because he didn't care. She hadn't believed him, not when it was so obvious that he cared about so many things, that he was still hurting from the horrors he'd witnessed through his work. But even knowing he was a good, caring man inside was not reason enough to risk everything.

"I'm sorry," she said helplessly. Confusion and pain blurred her mind. She couldn't think straight any more.

"Love or not, why don't you consider me instead of an anonymous donor, Erin? I'm afraid I don't know my exact IQ, but I'm very willing to provide both the sperm and information about my shoe size, as well as any other statistics your heart desires. I'll even throw in a conception that's a hell of a lot more fun than what you have in mind."

His sarcasm was too much.

"You are, are you?" she shouted. "You are willing to give me a baby and promise to leave us alone? If I could trust any man to do that, I would already have my baby."

"Are you living in a fairy tale, Erin? Have you even considered how difficult it is raising a child alone?"

"There are many women who manage just fine."

"Of course they manage. People do their best whenever there is no alternative. Unfortunately there are plenty of men who don't want to take responsibility for their children. But is it fair to the children, or their mothers?" He looked as if he'd like to shake her. "There is a reason why nature provides two parents for each child."

"I have my brother and sister to help. My parents."

"Have you thought about how it will feel when your baby starts to smile, and you wonder where that dimple came from? Or maybe she shows musical talent and you'll wonder if there are musicians in her genetic line." He grabbed her upper arms. "And when she asks, Erin, when she asks about her daddy, what are you going to tell her?"

Her voice was hoarse as her incoherent thoughts spilled forward in a mass of confused words. "I want children, but no man will have the right to take them away from me whenever he wants to play dad. No man will try to buy my children's love with sweets or toys or trips that I can't afford to give them." Her voice broke and to her horror she was viewing Nathan through a fog of tears. She lifted her hands up when he reached for her again. "Don't touch me, Nathan!"

He ignored her plea, and wrapped his arms around her, forcing her head against his shoulder. Her wet cheeks dampened the cotton, making it even darker. "It's OK, Erin. Come on. Your parents screwed up, but that is no reason to take such an extreme action. You're smart enough to know that yours was an extreme case. You are not your mother, and you know that all men aren't like your father.''

''That's not a risk I'm willing to take,'' she hiccuped, pushing him away even as she felt an almost irresistible longing to wrap her arms around his neck. She hated the helpless feeling that she was fleeing the unknown, escaping from something that could have been. ''Just leave me alone! I don't want you to mess up my life!'' She stumbled to the door, fumbled until she found the handle and escaped.

Despite the pain in her heart and the turmoil in her mind, she made it to work without so much as running over a single paperboy. Not that it did her much good. All she had done this morning was toy with a pencil and stare sightlessly at the computer screen. Her in-tray held enough assignments for a week, but she couldn't summon the resources needed to concentrate on her work.

She stared morosely at the screen, the screensaver blowing bubbles her way. Nathan had been furious and hurt. She ground her teeth at the thought. With her selfish thoughtlessness, she had hurt Nathan.

There would be no more renegotiations, no jokes and dry wit, no more "Miss Librarian." She swallowed. The nickname might be the thing she would miss the most.

Painful as this was, it was for the best, she reminded herself. It had to happen sooner or later. His finding out in this manner saved them from uncomfortable goodbyes. She had been weak, she had allowed herself to be with him, perhaps precisely because she knew he would soon be leaving again. It had felt good to have one day a week with him. She had pushed everything aside because being with him had just felt so darn good.

But now it was over.

It would hurt for a while. It would hurt to meet Nathan at his sister's house, but not too much damage had been done. They hadn't had a real relationship. Although Nathan seemed to think they had, she remembered with a sting. He had sounded hurt.

What a mess.

She doodled randomly on a pad, trying to gather her thoughts and calm down. It was time to move forward. Her plans had been well underway before she had even met Nathan Chase. She would be pregnant soon, and, if everything went well, this time next year she would have her baby. She took a deep breath. She'd have to stop being so stressed. Her baby would not benefit from her stress hormones flooding its system. She needed to calm down, to get her life back on track.

Nathan's baby. His sarcastic offer echoed in her ears. Had he meant it? She could have Nathan's baby.

She could not deny that in its impossibility the idea was tempting. She stabbed the writing pad with her pen, still doodling. Nathan would have been an excellent candidate for a one-night stand, resulting in a child he would never need to know about. Unethical as that was, she was desperate enough for a baby that she might have allowed that to happen.

But Nathan was family. If on a distant level, through Thomas and Sally he would always be a part of her life. It was impossible for her to have his child without his knowing and un-thinkable to allow him to father her child, even if his sarcastic offer was genuine. It would be the worst thing that could happen. Not only would her own tiny family be in danger, but also her extended family and even her brother's.

"Erin, these are email queries from this week." Mrs Appleton added a floppy disk to the pile in her in-tray. Reluctantly entering the computer age, the older woman grudgingly read the library's email but did not trust "advanced" features like forwarding.

"Ah, Nathan? So it's getting serious with you two?" With a broad smile she winked at Erin. "I like that one. Charming devil. I'm so glad I brought the two of you together."

Horrified, Erin glanced down at her pad, seeing Nathan's name written dozens of times. She tore the page off the pad and quickly ripped it to shreds.

Mrs Appleton chuckled. "No need to be embarrassed, my dear. I've been married over forty years now, but I still remember the intoxication of young love. I'm so glad you finally found someone special. It was about time."

She patted Erin on the shoulder before turning back to her desk.

Erin clenched her fists around the scraps of paper. Her heart was racing as it at last blasted its message through to her fiercely protesting brain.

I am not in love with Nathan, she chanted, *I am not in love. I like him, I want him, but I don't love him.* She opened her fist over the waste-paper basket, brushing her hands together until all the scraps had fluttered down. Her palm bore blue streaks from the ink. She rushed to the tiny bathroom, washing her hands until the skin was red.

The mirror reflected the image of a terrified woman. Shaking, she stared back at the pale ghost in the mirror, unable to deny the truth any longer. She had denied her feelings even to herself but the answer was now staring her in the face from the small mirror, radiating right alongside the terror. This was something she had never thought would happen. She had really thought she was immune to the virus they called love. In her arrogance she had let her defences down, and inch by inch Nathan had burrowed into her heart.

Somehow, the day passed. With vehement determination she concentrated on her work, ignored the frantic messages of fear and longing that her heart and brain exchanged, each struggling to convince the other.

She took her time leaving, postponing going home. At half-past four when she left the building the weather matched her mood; the dark sky was uninviting and in the streets snow had turned to gray sludge. Not knowing where to go, she trudged down the stairs feeling lost.

If she went back home she would either have to face Nathan or an empty house full of memories and the echoes of his laughter, and neither prospect appealed to her.

''Hello, Erin.''

He was leaning against the car, dressed in black, a woolen scarf loosely thrown around his neck. The smile was there, faint, but it was there. Erin came to a stop a few feet away from him, unable to help herself from devouring him with her eyes.

Nathan. This was the man she loved, his face serious and drawn despite the small smile as he waited for her response. She thrust her hands in her coat pockets and squared her shoulders. Now that she had admitted to herself that she loved him it was difficult to face him, to keep breaking down the bridge he kept building between them. Her heart was pushing her towards him, wanting her to do all kinds of silly things, such as run towards him, to throw herself into his arms and make him promise to keep her safe forever.

"I didn't expect to see you today," she said.

She was close enough now to see that the smile did not quite reach his eyes. "It's Friday."

"I thought the deal was off."

He opened the door for her. "Come on. Let's go. It's freezing out here."

His car was warm, but she hardly felt the difference. He drove silently for a while, heading out of the city.

"Where are we going?"

Nathan took one hand off the wheel and put it on her knee. "I don't know, Erin. I thought we were heading somewhere, but now I don't know any more."

"I was just asking where you were taking me," she muttered. "I wasn't speaking metaphorically."

Without answering, Nathan turned soon into a side-road and stopped at the edge of a forest. With the engine off, the silence in the car was almost claustrophobic. Out here the trees were still blanketed by snow. The scene looked like a Christmas card and she was painfully reminded of their playful kisses in the snow, of her snowbabies.

Without preamble he turned to her, his leather jacket crackling against the seat belt. ''If you really want to have a child now, why don't you consider having my baby?''

Shocked anew, she shook her head. Gone from his voice was the sarcasm, the anger. In its place was something else. Something much more dangerous.

Hesitation. Uncertainty. Hope.

''We're good together, Erin. I meant what I said this morning. Why don't you allow me to father this child, instead of a stranger?''

''Why? Why would you do that? What's in it for you?''

A muscle worked in his jaw. ''I would have a family of sorts. You and our child.''

''Families are overrated,'' she groaned. ''You don't understand. The reason I'm doing it this way is to avoid a family. And you—you can't even handle your own family. Your sister.''

Nathan sighed. ''Keep Sally out of this, Erin. I think we should give it a try.''

She shook her head, her throat too tight now for words.

Nathan spoke slowly. "I always thought I wasn't cut out to have real relationships, but it's been different with you. I...I care for you. We have a chance of making things work. Maybe it wouldn't ever be a real family, but if you're going to have a child, he or she should have a father. Why not me?"

He cared for her. Sensing how difficult that admission was for him, she nevertheless forced out the words. "No. No. This is such a mess. This Friday thing was all a big mistake."

"A mistake?"

"Yes. Nathan, how can you say you want us to be a family? You said you didn't need anyone. You ignore your own family as it is. What kind of parents do you think we'd make? You wouldn't even be there. You're never even in the country."

The silence stretched taut between them until she felt like screaming. Why didn't he explain? What had kept him away for all this time?

"OK. So you are saying that you don't want a relationship with me?" His voice was low and calm, matter-of-fact, but his features were hard, his eyes flaming.

Her heart bleeding, Erin nodded. He was ignoring her question. She didn't know the reasons for Nathan's behavior, but she had hoped he would confide in her. She didn't quite know what that would change, but it was something she needed to hear.

His lips narrowed into a thin line. "OK. Got it. And you'd rather have a baby by a stranger than by me?"

"Right," she croaked.

Nathan blew out a frustrated breath and hit the steering wheel with his fist. "What have we been doing these past few weeks, Erin? Was I just a toy to you? A distraction?"

"No, Nathan." Her voice broke again, and she fumbled for a tissue in her coat pocket. Nathan flipped open the glove compartment and tossed a small tissue pack in her lap. With angry movements, he rolled down the window as if to put some space between them. The breeze of icy air helped her to compose herself.

"When you started…well…'courting' me, as you put it, I couldn't resist. I allowed myself to be with you. I knew you wouldn't stay long, so I thought there was no harm in…" Her voice trailed off.

"Playing with me?" His voice was hard.

"If that's how you want to put it."

"But if we are talking trying for anything long-term, you don't want to have anything to do with me, baby or not. You don't even want to give it a try."

It was a statement, not a question.

Erin tried to swallow the lump in her throat. "My baby will be cousin to your niece. I don't want to complicate things." She swallowed, aware that she was about to say a hurtful thing. "I just want you to leave me alone."

Nathan tapped the steering wheel with his thumbs. His profile was hard as he stared towards the horizon. She thought he was about to say something, but then he started the car without a word.

"Would you take me back to the library, please?" she managed to ask when she noticed he was on the way back to the house. "I need to get Sabrina."

"Sabrina?"

"My car."

That almost got a raw chuckle, but the rest of the drive was silent. As the car rolled to a stop, she turned to him.

"You won't say anything, will you?" The words tumbled out, desperate yet wretched.

''To Thomas and Sally, I mean. They'll be home tomorrow and I'll go back to my apartment on Monday. You won't say anything, will you? About…us, or about my…about the baby?''

Nathan didn't even look at her. He opened his mouth to speak, but then seemed to change his mind. He shook his head, staring grimly forward.

Just managing to hold the tears back, she grappled with the door and escaped the confines of the car filled with his anger. As she reached Sabrina, she heard the roaring of his car as it sped away.

It was over.

Erin slid into her car and exhaled slowly, wrapping her arms around herself.

It was over now, and he had promised not to reveal her secret. Things had turned out in the best way possible.

Then why was she in agony, instead of being relieved?

The alarm went off in pitch-darkness, only minutes after she had managed to fall asleep. Yawning, she got dressed.

Nathan hadn't come home. His jacket was not slung over the chair by the kitchen door; his coffee-cup was not in the sink; his shoes didn't block the door; and his car was nowhere to be seen. With a heavy heart, Erin started her own car and drove to the airport. She tried not to think of where Nathan had spent the night. Just as she had wanted, it was none of her business.

Thomas and Sally looked refreshed and happy as she greeted them. Natalie was fast asleep on her father's shoulder. Erin kissed her plump cheek as she hugged her brother and sister-in-law. Her niece had inherited her father's complexion and her little face was covered in freckles.

"How was Greece?"

"Great!" Sally said at the same time as Thomas said,

"Wet."

Sally giggled. "Well, this isn't exactly the sunniest season over there. It was a bit rainy, but it was amazing anyway."

Thomas smiled indulgently, but pretended to send his wife a grim look. "We spent a whole day on the Acropolis. I've never been so soaked in my life! I didn't think I'd ever get dry again.''

Sally rolled her eyes. ''Don't you have any respect? What's a little rain when you were walking in the footsteps of Socrates and Plato?''

''I bet the buildings had roofs back then,'' Thomas grumbled good-naturedly. ''And I bet your Socrates would not have considered it wise to stand around in the rain gaping in awe at some old pieces of rock!''

''Don't listen to him. We went on a day-tour to Delphi. You know, where the oracle was? The tour guide told us...''

Sally's monologue on the way home on everything from Greek gods to Greek food saved Erin from having to take part in the conversation. Her muttered one-syllable words were enough.

''I can't wait to see Nathan.'' Sally moved restlessly in her seat as they approached their neighborhood. ''It's been almost two years since I saw him last. He still hasn't seen Natalie. Didn't he want to come with you to pick us up?''

''I'm sorry, Sally, I didn't think to ask. I didn't want to disturb him so early,'' Erin lied.

She hadn't thought of this. She hoped Nathan would be home to greet his sister. If he had moved out, or, God forbid, left the country, she had some explaining to do.

Nathan's black car was parked outside the house. Relieved, she parked next to it. Sally jumped out, picked up the sleeping Natalie in the car seat and rushed ahead of them into the house.

Thomas chuckled as they retrieved the luggage. "She really idolizes that brother of hers."

"She does. Have you ever met him?"

"Just twice. Once when we had just started dating, after their mother died. He stopped for a weekend at their father's house. And then he dropped by overnight when we had just moved in. Sally was pregnant then." He shrugged. "He seemed nice enough. Friendly, but a bit distant, more like a stranger than a family member. I don't think he quite realizes just how much Sally looks up to him." Thomas's voice turned rueful. "I have sometimes wondered if I will ever manage to live up to Big Brother."

Erin smiled at her brother. The three siblings were very close, having formed a separate alliance against their parents, instead of joining one of them. The age difference was so small that Thomas had always been more like the third twin than a big brother.

"Sally loves you, Tom. She doesn't want you running off to the edge of the world."

"What was your impression of Nathan? You've been living with him for a month, so you probably know him better than Sally does by now."

"He's OK," she answered vaguely, pocketing her keys and pushing the door open. "He doesn't seem to be rushing off this time, so you'll probably get to know him in the next few days."

Inside, Sally had thrown herself at Nathan and placed her daughter in his arms. Nathan was awkwardly patting his sister's back, smiling down at her as she chatted. He gave Erin a neutral nod, and shook hands with Thomas.

Erin excused herself to her room as quickly as she could without offending anyone and stayed there. Only when she heard Sally call out a loud goodbye to her brother did she venture back downstairs and into the living room, where Sally was changing her daughter on the floor.

Sally looked slyly up at her. "So, how was living with Nathan?"

Erin gave her sister-in-law a dry glance. Her matchmaking efforts were neither forgiven nor forgotten. "Nathan was no trouble," she replied shortly. "He's housebroken."

Sally wasn't about to be brushed off. "Did the two of you hit it off?" Her green eyes, almost the same shade of intense green as Nathan's, were wide open in anticipation. "I mean...any...romance in the air?"

"Nope."

Sally's face fell. "That's too bad. I thought you might make a terrific couple." She sighed and stared wistfully at Erin. "I thought it would be so romantic. Two people, both emotionally scarred, both determined never to let anyone close, finding love when forced together by circumstances."

Erin rolled her eyes. "Sally, you watch too many soppy movies." Curiosity got the better of her. "Why do you say Nathan is emotionally scarred?"

Sally picked her daughter up. "Why do you want to know?"

"Sally." Her voice was pleading, and her sister-in-law relented.

"OK. Come into the kitchen and sit down."

At the kitchen table, her hands wrapped around a hot cup of coffee, Erin waited for her sister-in-law to explain. Sally was quiet as she poured herself a cup of coffee, obviously gathering her thoughts.

"What did you think of Nathan?" she then asked, and Erin fought to keep herself from blushing.

"He's different from what I expected," she said cautiously.

Sally smiled. "I know you think he's been cruel to me, not coming home more often," she said and Erin started in surprise. She'd thought she'd kept her anger well hidden. "But I understand why. I can't say he hasn't hurt my feelings once or twice, but considering what he's been through I can understand that he stays away."

Erin just waited. This was sounding more and more intriguing.

"Nathan doesn't have good memories of our family, and I was just a kid when he left home." She shrugged. "It's not really a secret, we just don't talk about it. Nathan is not my biological brother. He was adopted when he was five."

"Adopted?" Erin stared at her. "He can't be adopted—the two of you look so much alike!" The green eyes and dark hair—even the coloring was similar.

Sally nodded. "I know. But that's just a coincidence, I'm afraid. Our parents thought they couldn't have children, so they adopted him. He had been shuffled between foster homes for a while." She sighed. "Then three years later, when Nathan was eight years old, I came along. They were so happy that they forgot they already had a little boy. They didn't mean to, and they never mistreated him or anything like that, but they all but forgot him. That, on top of his biological parents abandoning him, must have been terrible."

Erin clenched her fists as she remembered the hard look on Nathan's face as he'd asked her what would happen to her sperm-bank baby if she later had children with someone she loved. "You'd be amazed at human nature," he'd said.

Erin's heart ached for the little boy, losing his parents for the second time. Was this why he had stayed away from his sister? Did he still resent her for taking his place in their parents' hearts?

"Even I felt it," Sally continued, a wretched frown marring her brow. "And I was just a child myself. And of course Nathan felt it. He stayed out of the way when he felt he wasn't wanted."

"Was he upset with you?"

"Me?" Sally blinked, then laughed. "Oh, you mean was he jealous of me? I suppose he must have been, on some level, but he never let on. He moved away when I was only ten, and he is eight years older so we were never very close. But he's always been very good to me."

A few weeks ago, Erin would have pointed out that sending postcards and calling his sister twice a year was hardly the most affectionate attitude in the world. She didn't now. She could only imagine the terrible hurt his parents had inflicted on him, the certainty he must have felt about being unlovable.

"Did he ever meet his birth parents?"

Sally nodded. "As I understand it, he lived with them until he was three, when Social Services took him away because they neglected him. I don't think he remembers much from that time, but he found them when he was around seventeen, just before he moved away.

The mother threw a beer bottle at him, screaming that he had ruined her life. The father was nice enough, but his primary concern was preventing Nathan from spilling the beans to his new family.''

''I see,'' Erin murmured, deep in thought.

''Of course, after this,'' Sally pointed to her framed magazine cover on the wall, ''both of them came crawling, thinking he must have plenty of money to throw around.'' She put her hand on Erin's arm. ''Nathan never talks about his biological parents. The only reason I even know is that I went with him when he visited his birth mother. I was nine and hid in the back of his car.''

Erin's heart was still bleeding. ''It's amazing that he turned out so well,'' she said.

Sally nodded. ''I'm so proud of my brother,'' she said. ''I just wish he'd find the perfect woman and fall in love. I would like to see him happy. He's always so restless.'' She turned her attention back to Erin. ''Not even a hint of attraction?'' she asked with a dejected sigh.

Erin shook her head, but the tint in her cheeks immediately lifted Sally's spirits.

"There was!" she exclaimed in triumph. "I knew it!" She moved her chair closer to Erin and put an arm over her shoulder. "Tell me all about it!"

Despite her pain, Erin couldn't help laughing. "There is nothing to tell, Sally." She changed the subject. "I heard Thomas is on the phone with Mom right now. Has Mom or Dad talked to you about Christmas yet?"

Sally shrugged. "I leave those things to Thomas. He's more of a diplomat than I am. I would just tell them to think of someone other than themselves for a while." She looked up, contrite. "Sorry."

Erin gave a small smile. "Don't be. I know how they are."

"We are still determined to be here this Christmas, what with Nathan here and all. Erika's coming. We'd be very happy if you'd stay also. And, of course, we're going to invite both your parents to stay with us, if they want."

Erin hesitated. It was tempting to break away from the series of dysfunctional Christmases. This was her chance. Both Thomas and Erika were making a stand. If she didn't do this now, she could be stuck in the same rut for all eternity, spending half of each holiday with each parent. Eating two dinners, just because neither would give in. She shook her head. The three of them had really been cowards to let it go on so long. Somehow it had just become a ritual, ever since they were kids. It was time for it to end.

But staying here would also mean spending Christmas with Nathan.

Thomas walked in, shaking his head. ''One down, one to go. She is not a happy lady.''

''Aw,'' Sally said, patting her husband's knee as he sat down on the couch. ''I'm sorry.''

Thomas shrugged. ''She doesn't want to come, of course.'' He looked at his sister. ''Erin, she wanted to speak with you, but I told her you weren't here right now. I thought you'd appreciate a chance to make up your mind without her breathing down your neck.''

''They'll be hurt,'' Erin muttered, too stricken with anxiety to remember to thank her brother for his thoughtfulness.

''They won't be hurt, Erin,'' Thomas said derisively. ''They will sulk for a while, but they won't be hurt. This is just about winning over the other one. That's how it always has been. And it's not as though they will be spending Christmas alone. They both have their families, and besides, the offer for them to come and spend Christmas with us is very genuine.''

They did have their own families. Their mother had a new husband and the twins. Their father had a girlfriend who was Thomas's age and they were raising her two children along with three-year-old Alexandra.

''I'll miss the kids,'' Erin said wistfully. She had already made up her mind. She wouldn't continue participating in her parents' game.

''I took care of that too,'' Thomas said proudly. ''I invited the kids to Natalie's birthday on the twenty-seventh.''

''All of them?'' Erin laughed. ''Won't it be a riot in a few years when the twins and Alexandra decide to become best friends?''

Thomas chuckled. ''Yeah. I think riot is an appropriate word.''

Erin sighed. Christmas was just around the corner, and it was nothing but a heap of trouble.

CHAPTER SEVEN

EVEN with the usual hectic Christmas schedule, and her parents' outrage at hearing her decision, the days dragged on. In the end, her parents had sullenly accepted the three siblings' decision, but both had declined the offer to spend Christmas at Thomas's house. In itself, that was also a relief. Perhaps things would be easier from now on.

Every other day or so, letters dropped in her mailbox, containing some of Nathan's photographs and curt but detailed suggestions as to what they could portray. She had been stunned when the first one arrived, to see that he intended to follow through on their project. But then she did the same. Although lacking in any decent enthusiasm now, she wrote short passages, clipped them to the photographs and sent them back to him along with suggestions of her own, feeling ridiculous as she wrote his name and the address in block letters so Thomas or Sally wouldn't recognize her handwriting. Neither of them had mentioned their project, so presumably Nathan hadn't told them about it yet. And while everything was so uncertain, she didn't want them to know either.

The sharp pain of losing him did not go away. She even felt foolish for thinking in those terms. She'd never had Nathan—so she hadn't lost him. She'd made a decision that was for the best. It would be for the best. For both of them, and for her baby.

When I have my baby, she promised herself. *Everything will be just fine once my baby is here.* And she would have to learn to deal with Nathan occasionally. It was unlikely that he would often be around, but she would have to be able to talk with him casually, smile at him as if they were friendly acquaintances. In a little while they might even be able to finish that darn book together and become nothing more than amicable in-laws.

In time.

And too soon, all too soon, it was Christmas, and with dread Erin drove towards her brother's house for lunch, her own pile of presents stacked high on the back seat.

Nathan's car was outside the house, reminding her what waited inside, and she sat for long minutes in her own car, trying to work up the courage to go inside. Although she had frequently visited over the past few weeks, she had been careful to limit those visits to times when it was unlikely that he would be there, and was quick to drive right past the house should the black sports car unexpectedly be parked outside.

When her windows began to fog up she finally roused herself, picked up the presents from the back seat and let herself in, using her own key as Sally had instructed.

Nathan was the first person she saw, and she ate him up with her eyes in the few seconds before he noticed she was there. Knowing about his painful background had made him even more precious to her, added to her love a longing to heal his wounds, to hold him and keep him safe, the same feelings she'd felt surge when he'd told her about his work. A need to protect, and she couldn't do anything about any of it.

It hurt. All of it.

He was standing in the living room, leaning against a wall and smiling down at little Natalie, precariously balancing against his leg, her small hand clutching his fingers. Then he looked up and saw her. For a moment his eyes narrowed, then they went blank.

"Hello, Erin. Nice to see you again." He was smiling politely as he nodded towards her, as if nothing had ever happened between them. As if they'd never shared incredible kisses right on that couch; as if they'd never lain giggling together in a pile of snow; as if she'd never rejected him, pushed him away and told him she didn't want him.

For a moment she wondered if his polite manner meant that she had over-interpreted his reaction to her rejection. Then she realized he was doing what he had promised. He was being the perfect gentleman, and not allowing their personal history to shadow the family's Christmas. A rough feeling overtook her heart. He had promised, and he was keeping that promise. There wasn't so much as a hint of antagonism in his face, his behavior or his words.

Something clicked in her brain, and the world shifted into a different focus. Why had she automatically assumed Nathan would behave like her mother and father had? He wasn't. *She*, however, had avoided her brother's house for fear of running into him.

She was the one guilty of letting their personal relationship interfere with their family, not he. *She* was the one following in her parents' footsteps, not he.

Did that change anything?

She stared resolutely at his forehead as she returned his greeting and then turned away to say hello to Thomas and Sally. She knew she was being a coward, but one look into those emerald eyes across the room and she was afraid she wouldn't be able to keep anything from him. Not her surprise, her gratitude, her shame—or her love.

"Nathan is going away in a few days," Sally said with a small pout. "He's off again into the big, bad world."

"Really?" So, he was over his crisis, Erin thought. It hadn't taken long. Just as she had suspected, Nathan was going away.

"It's just a small trip," Nathan said. "Nothing big. I'll just be gone two or three weeks, then you'll have to put up with me again for a while. If you don't mind?"

"Of course not!" Sally hugged her brother, smiling up at him. "I love having you around. And I'm so glad that you've finally got to know Natalie and Thomas."

"So am I," Nathan replied. His return of his sister's embrace was somewhat awkward, but more graceful than the last hug she'd seen. Perhaps brother and sister had been practising. Accidentally, Erin met his eyes but looked away before he could perform his usual mind-reading trick.

"What a beautiful Christmas tree," she said with a smile. She had seen it before, but not decorated. The tree was tall, the star almost touching the ceiling. It was decorated with tiny green and red lights along with small glittering spheres in red and gold. Clashing with the overall picture, only paper ornaments decorated the lowest branches.

Sally noticed where she was looking. "Natalie always makes a beeline for the tree, so we can't have any breakables where she can reach," she explained with a tired grin, picking the little culprit up from the floor. "She crawls there at the speed of light, and when we pick her up her arms and legs just keep moving until we put her down again." She stroked her daughter's red hair affectionately. "She knows what she wants, this one."

Erin reached out towards little Natalie, who threw herself into her aunt's arms and babbled, hands waving towards the tree. Erin hugged her niece, inhaled the soft scent of a baby and felt the inner longing pull at her again.

"She's a handful, isn't she?" Nathan asked with a quirky smile. He was standing by the fireplace, a glass of wine in his hand. Erin's heart skipped a beat as she watched the lights on the tree cast a faint red hue on his dark hair, slightly damp. He could have just come from a shower, or been outside where snow was falling. A different kind of longing pulled at her insides.

Sally chuckled. "She certainly is, but she is worth it."

"It's amazing, isn't it, how some women manage to raise their children alone?" Nathan continued, ignoring the warning look Erin gave him as she lowered the child back to the floor.

Sally rolled her eyes. "Absolutely. Even if they have family who can help, it must be hell to go through all the sleepless nights without any support."

Nathan nodded. "And they can't stay at home with the baby either. They have to return to work to support themselves and the child."

"Well, at least they usually get some kind of financial support from the father."

"In this day and age, there isn't even always a father," Nathan commented. Erin had turned her back on him, obstinately watching little Natalie as she toddled towards her toy box, but she felt his gaze burn itself into the back of her head. She gritted her teeth. How dared he?

"And then there are the teenage years, with all sorts of new problems. It can't be easy for a single mother to handle all that."

Erin pivoted around. He was going too far. "Sometimes it can be better for a family just to have one parent," she interjected. "Sally, you've seen first-hand how things are between our parents, you know how they still fight over us."

Sally smiled sympathetically, but did not make a comment. "Well, the kitchen is calling. I will leave you two to discuss the problems of family." She paused in the doorway. "And, since we are on the subject, if you ask me, it is high time at least one of you provided my daughter with some cousins to play with!" She winked, and vanished giggling into the kitchen as her brother frowned at her.

Erin sat down on the floor next to her niece. She jumped to feel Nathan's hand on her shoulder. He had knelt down beside them.

"Is my sister going to get her wish in the new year, Erin?"

She wondered if the heat from his hand could burn a hole in her blouse. Muscles tense, she kept her eyes focused on her niece and tried to ignore the presence of the man beside her. "I hope so," she replied.

There was silence, except for Natalie's soft chatter as she piled blocks on top of each other.

"I miss you," Nathan breathed in her ear, his warmth and his scent so close that she had to clench all muscles to keep herself from turning to him, wrapping her arms around him and just sobbing until he promised her everything would be fine. "I even miss your barbed comments in the morning before you have your first cup of coffee. And I miss the way you look at me with a confused frown, biting your lip, whenever you've failed to convince yourself that there is nothing between us."

She squeezed her eyes shut. *Don't do this to me, Nathan. Please stay angry with me.*

His finger reached out and touched her temple, stroking gently down to her chin. He nudged her face towards him, but she kept her eyes averted. She hated the vulnerability he made her feel, hated the way she longed to just lean into his arms and trust him to make everything right.

"Do you miss me too?"

Erin bit her lip, both to keep a resounding yes from tumbling out and to keep the tears inside, just long enough to escape his penetrating attention. She mustn't lose sight of her goals. She mustn't. She glanced up to him, mouth opened to deny his question, but when their eyes met she couldn't move, couldn't speak. Had his eyes always been this green? His smile always this bitter-sweet?

God, Nathan, I miss you so much.

"There you are, sis! Ah, and the baby. My God, how she grows."

Erin jumped to her feet and hugged her sister with even more affection than usual, grateful for the interruption. Surreptitiously she wiped her eyes as Erika introduced herself to Nathan. He greeted her with his usual charm and then excused himself as Sally called his name from the kitchen.

"Wow, you were right, he is quite something," Erika whispered in Erin's ear, smiling as she stared after Nathan. "I could drown in those eyes. If you don't want him, I do."

Erin felt an unexpected pain at her twin's words. "What about Richard?" she asked, her voice brittle.

Her sister shrugged. "Richard doesn't have a monopoly over me. If I want someone else, there is nothing he can do about it," she said defiantly. Too defiantly. Erin knew her sister well. There was something different about her now.

Could her sister finally have met her match?

"So, sis. What will it be?" Erika asked brightly. "Just say the word. Is Nathan free game, or do you want him all to yourself?"

"I want him," Erin blurted out, not prepared to call Erika's bluff. She couldn't bear even the thought of her sister and Nathan together. "Hands off, sister. He's mine."

"I'm glad to hear it," Nathan drawled from the doorway, his eyes intent on her. "The feeling is entirely mutual."

While Erin searched the floor for a hole to crawl into, Erika clapped her hands in delight, then grabbed Nathan's hand and pulled him

towards Erin. "Come on, let me see a kiss.
I've never seen my sister being kissed."

Face burning, Erin shook her head vehe-
mently and put out a hand to hold Nathan
away as Erika pushed them together. "Forget
it, Erika, I'm not putting on a show for you."

"Come on..." Erika grabbed something
from her handbag and waved it over her head.
"I always carry mistletoe in my bag at
Christmas. You never know when it might
come in handy." She winked at Nathan.
"She's standing under the mistletoe. Make the
most of it."

"He's not..." Erin began, then stopped.
"Don't mind me," she muttered, dodging the
mistletoe. "I'll be in the corner over there,
mingling with the dust bunnies."

Suddenly her feet weren't touching the
ground any more.

Nathan's arms were around her waist, easily
holding her up to his height. For a second she
was looking into his eyes, her hands grabbing
his shoulders for support, then his mouth was
on hers and she forgot everything except the
warmth of his body, the strength of his arms
around her, the intoxicating taste and scent of
him. *I missed you*, her soul whispered to him,

inserting the unspoken message in every touch. *I missed you, I love you.* He felt so warm and alive and he was there, close, as she'd thought he'd never be again.

Long moments later, her feet touched the ground again. She opened her dazed eyes to see her sister theatrically fanning herself with a book.

"Wow! That was really something!" She winked at her sister. "You have my approval."

A man appeared in the doorway behind Erika, pushed by an enthusiastic Sally. "Your Richard is here, Erika!"

Erin had never before seen her sister speechless. She was staring at her boyfriend as if he'd suddenly grown a third eye. Having never met Richard herself, Erin decided to follow her example. He was about their age, with blond hair and warm brown eyes, dressed in black trousers and a thick knitted sweater. Faint traces around his eyes and mouth suggested frequent laughter and his smile was apologetic as he looked at Erika. All in all, he looked very different from Erika's usual type of boyfriend.

"I'm sorry to interrupt, Erika, but you left your keys at my place." He held up the articles in question.

"It's no interruption," Sally replied when there was no answer from Erika. "Why don't you stay for dinner? There's plenty of food and it is so terrific to finally meet Erika's man. Well…" she laughed "…I suppose I'm asking a bit late. You probably have people waiting for you?"

Unspoken messages travelled between Richard and Erika. Sensitive to her twin's mood, Erin reached out and squeezed her hand, finding it icy. She knew that her sister was terrified of emotional closeness and of letting anyone threaten the new and fragile family the sisters had formed with Thomas and Sally. Looking at the determined look on Richard's face, she suspected he knew exactly what he was doing.

"No…" He looked at Erika again. "I hoped I'd have plans, but they fell through. Thank you, I would love to stay."

Way to go, Richard, Erin secretly thought as she heard her sister's shocked indrawn breath.

Sally vanished into the kitchen, leaving the four of them standing awkwardly around. Erin glanced at her sister and worried for a moment she might faint, but she kept herself upright, still staring at Richard as if seeing a new species of ghost.

Richard finally tore his gaze from Erika and looked at Erin. His smile was forced. ''Erika told me that the two of you were identical twins, but you don't look that much alike. I would never have trouble recognizing who was who.''

Erin laughed. ''If we work at it, we can look alike, but only to strangers. Somehow our personalities turned out very different, and that always shines through.'' She reached out her hand. ''Nice to meet you at last, Richard. Erika has told me a lot about you.'' Richard's gaze flew to Erika even as he shook Erin's hand.

''She has?''

Erin winced as her sister's toe rammed her calf.

''And you must be Erin's Nathan,'' Richard added and nodded to Nathan. It was Erin's turn to be embarrassed over the other twin's revelations.

The two men shook hands, then fell into easy conversation, leaving the two sisters silent at their sides, glaring at each other and their men. It was almost funny, Erin thought, how she knew that the helpless panic she saw in her sister's face must be reflected in her own. Yet there were other things too in her sister's eyes. Hope, perhaps. Excitement.

After a few minutes, Nathan's arm went over her shoulder and his body to her side, reminding her of the public, but oh, so blissful, kiss they had so recently shared.

"Perhaps we should see if Sally needs some help," he suggested. Reluctant to leave her sister, who seemed almost paralyzed, Erin paused, but not for long. The two of them would have to work this out.

Busy thinking about her sister and Richard, she was surprised to find herself not in the kitchen, but in Thomas's office alone with Nathan. He pulled her into his arms, lifting her chin so their eyes met. "No more hiding, Erin. Give us a chance."

Her vocal cords refused to co-operate. Her mouth moved, but no words emerged. Then, before she realized what she was doing, she had nodded in agreement. Why not? He was going away in just a few days. Why not allow herself to be with the man she loved, just until he left? A few days. It would be worth it.

Wouldn't it? He'd already shown he was capable of keeping up the pretense in front of their family. She wouldn't have to worry about it turning ugly, and she wouldn't have to worry about a commitment. Just a few days of living for the present. Then she could go on with her life, and he'd only be a peripheral figure, an in-law. It could work. Couldn't it?

She realized she was frowning when he pulled one corner of her mouth upward with a finger. "Smile for me, Erin. I promise, it won't be that bad. I'll even floss, just for you."

Her giggle turned into a sob, but she hid it in the warmth of his shoulder. She held him tightly and he rocked her as if he sensed that she needed comfort. She was so confused. She wanted Nathan. She wanted to be with him, to touch him, to make love with him. But she wanted her baby too.

The baby was her future. Nathan couldn't be anything other than a temporary figure in her life. She'd have to be sure he realized that. He'd already offered to father her baby, and she'd have to make sure he realized that was not in the picture.

She raised her head and looked up into his eyes. "Don't say anything to Thomas or Sally, please, Nathan? That way there will be no problem when…''

His eyes were watchful. ''When what?''

''When you go away. There won't be anything to explain.''

''I won't be gone for long. I'll be back in just a few weeks.''

''Don't. You're leaving in just a few days. Can we just live in the present and not think about the future? Please? You're going away soon, let's just enjoy this time together.''

His fingers caressed the nape of her neck and his eyes were unreadable. ''And when I come back?''

She shook her head. ''We have a few days, Nathan. Nothing more. Neither of us could handle anything more, and I've already made plans for my future.''

He rubbed his nose against hers and held her gaze with his. ''We'll see what happens, OK? We have a few days together now, then I'm coming back and we'll see then.''

When you come back, if *you come back, I'll be pregnant with somebody else's baby,* she silently thought.

A sudden grin transformed Nathan's face, making him look carefree and arrogant instead of serious. It just made her sad. "And for the next few days I'm going to make sure you miss me as much as possible until I return."

She had to smile, but it was a sad one. She doubted he would even be coming back once he was on the road again. Not this man who'd stayed away from his only sister for years on end. She knew he had feelings for her, he even "might be" in love with her, but that wasn't enough. He was a wanderer at heart, not someone to trust in love or commitment, and she was the type to say better safe than sorry, someone who had never believed in relationships, and whose only attempt at one had ended in disaster. Regardless of how she felt about him, even how he felt about her, things between her and Nathan could never be more than fleeting.

But they did have a few days. A few days without the future hanging over their heads. She looked up at him. "Will you come home with me tonight, Nathan?"

He hesitated, searching her face. "Are you sure?"

She nodded. She was nervous, even somewhat scared of the big step they were about to take, a step that would change the nature of their relationship, but she was very sure. They deserved a few days and nights together before it ended.

To her surprise the look on his face stayed hesitant, then turned determined. "First we should talk, Erin."

Her arms wound around his neck as she brought her lips to his, gently brushing the corner of his mouth with the tip of her tongue. "No, Nathan. No talking tonight. There is plenty of time for talking later. Let's just feel. Not think or talk. Please?"

Beneath her hand on his neck, she felt his heart begin to race until it matched the speed of her own heart. She couldn't control the thrilled smile spreading over her face. If she had ever doubted that he wanted her, the hard pounding of his heart was proof enough.

"So you're finally going to admit you like me, Librarian?" he murmured against her mouth, his lips curving against hers. She giggled back, frowning at him in mock-irritation.

"You finally broke me, hotshot. I'll admit it. I like you." She sealed the admission with a kiss and this time their enthusiasm was unhampered by a crowd of onlookers.

Nathan groaned and reluctantly pulled away from her. He sighed and ran a hand through his hair, mussing it even further. ''We have a whole day of family stuff to get through.''

His wretched tone was unbelievably flattering. She felt sexy and wanted, not to mention even more determined that this man would be firmly entrenched in her bed tonight.

Floating, she got through the rest of the day on fantasies and anticipation, pushing reality far away, a wide smile stretching her lips every time she caught Nathan's hot gaze across the room.

Then finally, finally they could leave. Having hatched quite an elaborate plot, Erin moaned about the bad tires on her car and the state of the roads this time of year, and Nathan immediately offered to drive her home. Sally's gaze moved back and forth between them, a small smile hovering on her lips, and Erin had the scary feeling she wasn't fooled and wouldn't be waiting up for her brother.

As she sat down in the familiar interior of Nathan's car she felt an overwhelming feeling of rightness. The man she loved was at her side, and soon she would know him in every way a woman could know a man.

Nathan trailed a finger across her knee and smiled at her, his features tense. She circled his wrist with her fingers and rubbed her thumb back and forth over his pulse, revelling in watching his eyes darken even further. At last he withdrew his hand and inserted the key in the ignition, then hesitated. His gaze searched her face for a second. "I just thought of something. Do you have any protection at your place?"

She shook her head, blushing faintly. "I wasn't planning this," she muttered.

"I suppose there must be an open pharmacy *somewhere...*" Nathan mused, "even on Christmas Day."

"Well," Erin muttered, "I did notice there were some upstairs in the guest bathroom."

She was rewarded by a quick kiss on her nose. "You're a genius. I'll be right back."

Nathan ran inside the house, leaving her shivering with nervous anticipation. The primary feeling was happiness. She was going to ignore all those other feelings, all the doubt and fear. He would be going away so soon. There was plenty of time for heartbreak then. For a few days she just wanted to be happy and carefree. She knew there would never be regrets, but there would be heartbreak. This time, the memories would be worth it. They already were.

Nathan came back shaking his head, looking uncharacteristically embarrassed as he plodded through the snow towards the car. Sliding into his seat with a big sigh, he gestured towards the house.

"Sally caught me red-handed getting this from the bathroom cabinet," he said with a lopsided grin, showing her the small box before throwing it into his camera bag in the back seat. "It was all she could do not to cheer us on."

Erin hid her face in her hands. "She didn't?"

"She sends her warmest regards."

Erin slid down in her seat and peeked over to the house. Sure enough, there was Sally, waving excitedly from the window. Seeing Erin look her way, she gave her the thumbs-up.

Erin whimpered and slid as low as the seat belt would allow. With a rueful chuckle, Nathan started the car and pulled away from the house.

"I can't believe she knows what we are going to do," she groaned.

Nathan reached out to pat her knee. "Don't worry, sweetheart. We'll do things she couldn't possibly imagine."

She peered sideways at him. "I hate to break this to you, Nathan, but your little sister is not a complete innocent. She does have a child. Do you know how babies are made? She certainly does. There's a small red-headed proof."

Nathan winced. "Don't. She's still my baby sister. And anyway, it doesn't matter, I *still* plan on quite a few things anyone would have trouble imagining. I've had much too much time to fantasize for the past few weeks."

Erin laughed at his mock-arrogance. She felt free, now that her mind was made up. She allowed herself to devour Nathan's face with her eyes as he drove through the starry night. He looked happy, his eyes warm with smiles and anticipation as he glanced her way.

Once inside her apartment, Nathan spent a minute getting reacquainted with Your Boyfriend and Your Girlfriend. She showed him the small apartment, leaving the kitchen for last. She didn't want to end with the bedroom. It seemed too obvious.

Not that their purpose in coming here hadn't been obvious for all, she ruefully remembered.

"This is the bedroom," she announced, opening the door and switching on the lights. She then moved across the hall to the kitchen door. "And the kitchen is here…"

Nathan hadn't followed.

"I don't think we need to explore any further tonight," he said quietly.

Erin hesitated, then turned the kitchen light off.

He held out his hand. "Come here, Librarian."

Soft, oh, so soft, seductive voice. Warm gaze…no, more than warm, hot, searing, blazing, scorching, sizzling, all those things he had once suggested, almost burning her with its intensity. She moved closer, pulled towards him by an intangible force that wrapped around the two of them, enveloping them inside their own private universe. She was aching to touch him, to experience all of him. It was about time. She laughed, a liberating sound that expelled any remaining doubt that she was doing the right thing.

"Ah, Erin," Nathan breathed as his arms went around her in a tight hug. "You are the best Christmas present ever." He backed towards the bed and sat down with her in his lap. "Can I unwrap you now?"

Erin couldn't get enough of just looking at him, touching him, feeling his warmth under her fingertips. *Finally!* her heart was singing. She pushed him on his back and lay on top of him, kissing his face and neck. His heart thumped beneath her hands as she ran them over him, for the moment secure and confident in the knowledge of his hunger for her. His smile was intoxicating. Moments passed, hours for all she knew, and their clothes vanished piece by piece until they could finally touch each other fully, and the feel of his body against hers was more amazing than she'd ever have believed.

As they touched and caressed each other he kept whispering soft and sexy words in her ear, and she couldn't help but squirm in smiling embarrassment, her cheeks burning, as she giggled at his teasing attempts to shock her. He grinned at her, then the ghost of a smile laced his kisses as his mouth explored her body. And as she forgot any remaining timidity he encouraged her to touch him, led the way and then gently commanded her to lead, never allowing her to doubt her ability to please him. And when they finally did come together there was only white, soaring pleasure, a sense of completion, of perfection, of being one. It was *right.*

The only detraction from her enjoyment was the muzzle on her mouth, the absolute necessity of not slipping. She could not, *could* not, tell him how much she loved him, even when he smiled so tenderly into her eyes, his expression telling her so much about how precious she was to him despite their situation. She could not allow those words to leave her mouth, those thoughts that were all that filled her mind, so all she could do was chant his name over and over again, then cry it out as he drove her over the brink. And in return, she heard her own name explode in her ear.

Nothing would ever be the same again.

"Erin?"

The bed was warm, and just a few seconds before she'd been hugging this huge, warm teddy bear. She didn't want to open her eyes. She wanted her teddy bear back in her arms where he belonged. It had been most rude of him to go away.

"I want to take your picture, Erin. OK?"

That woke her up. "My picture?" She opened her eyes to see Nathan sitting on the bed holding his camera. Her eyes opened wide in shock. "You are most certainly not taking any naked pictures of me!" she cried out, clutching the covers to her neck.

Nathan shook his head. "Not naked. Under the covers, sleepy and beautiful." He kissed her gently, feathering kisses over her face and hair. "OK?"

She could only nod, the tender look in his eyes melting her completely.

Almost falling asleep again, she dreamily obeyed Nathan's gentle commands as he moved around her, snapping pictures. He probably should have looked a bit silly, she thought, snapping pictures in the nude, but he didn't. Or if he did, he looked adorably silly.

"Nathan?"

"Mmm…?"

"What are you going to do with those pictures?"

He snapped a few more before answering. "Nothing. I just wanted to capture the way you looked when I woke up this morning.'' His voice sounded wistful. ''I'll give them to you,'' he added.

Bemused, Erin realized that instead of suffering through an embarrassing morning-after scene, she was posing for her lover's camera, even if only from beneath the covers.

He had to have bewitched her. That was the only explanation, logical or not.

Nathan put the camera away, then lay down on top of her, his head at her midriff.

''Good morning,'' he said, smiling. ''Thank you for last night.''

His eyes were warm, the green flames reaching out to caress her. Erin grinned as she stretched, then reached out to run a hand over his bare shoulder, connecting again. ''Any time,'' she muttered. His eyes lit up, and only then she realized what she had said. She groaned and grabbed a pillow to cover her face.

Nathan didn't object to the pillow. Instead he pulled on the sheet until he had uncovered the rest of her, and when his warm hands and mouth were on her again it was impossible to keep hiding behind the pillow. She reached out to him, to touch him in return, but he gently took her wrists, and moved them away. "Enjoy," he whispered. "I want to please you."

Enjoy she did. Feeling deliciously depraved, she lay there as his warm hands and his wicked mouth explored every inch of her body. Beneath half-closed eyelids, she revelled in watching what he was doing to her body, in meeting his heated gaze.

When he finally moved over her, she was already at the edge. Her hands clenched his shoulders frantically as she hovered on the brink. She couldn't believe it when he stopped.

"Nathan…?"

He held his body still, trapping her under his weight so that she couldn't move against him. Green fire burned into her eyes as he supported himself on his elbows and stared down at her face, his gaze intense and determined.

"Have my baby, Erin."

Afterwards she lay draped over him, her eyes closed, exhausted, but holding on to the wondrous sensation that lingered despite the lurking unease. She didn't want to think about anything yet. Especially not his suggestion.

Nathan, however, held a different perspective. Spent, she tried to ignore his words and just listen to the timbre of his voice and enjoy the feeling of his hands moving up and down her back, but when he began listing prospective baby names she had to stop him.

"We're not having a baby, Nathan!"

His hand only paused for a moment, then continued. "Of course we are, sweetheart. You said yes, remember?"

"I did not!" Erin cried.

"Yes, you did, sweetheart," Nathan said reasonably. "To be precise, you said 'Yes, Nathan, yes, oh, please…'"

Erin noticed that blushing wasn't restricted to the face after all. With a mixture of annoyance, embarrassment and something she refused to acknowledge as regret, she sat up, wrapping the sheets around her body. "I don't think I was in a fit state to reply to your question. I'll have to plead temporary insanity." She stared at him, the glint in his eyes telling her he wasn't taking her seriously. "You can't seduce someone into agreeing to have your baby, Nathan."

"I just did," he pointed out.

"It's not happening. You being the father of my baby would complicate everything. Neither of us wants commitment or a relationship. I just want a quiet, simple life, just me and my baby. Nobody else. And if you'd stop obsessing about this, you'd realize how crazy it would be. For both of us.''

She looked down to see if her words were hurting him. Clearly they were not. He was smiling dreamily, eyes half-lidded. His hand reached towards her, covering her belly. ''Why not me, rather than some nameless guy you'll never meet? I can't see a single reason why this baby, for better or worse, can't inherit my shoe size and IQ, not some anonymous geek's.''

He sounded possessive. Erin closed her eyes in aggravation. ''Nathan, you are not listening to me!''

''That's because you are not making any sense, my darling.'' He dragged her back down and kissed the base of her throat. ''Intelligent as you are, you lose all perspective when it comes to that baby you have your mind set on.''

He pulled her back on top of him, maneuvering her until she was straddling him. ''I'm very open-minded, Erin. I'm even ready to make the baby right here and now.''

She could tell he was. Before his hands could get too adventurous she wriggled off him.

"We are most definitely not making a baby. I'm taking a bath while you come to your senses," she muttered, escaping into the bath-room and locking the door. Her spinning head needed time to settle down and it would be just like Nathan to join her uninvited.

On the other side of the door, she heard him chuckle. She tried not to think about him as she ran a bath, and waited impatiently for the tub to fill. After tossing in some lavender bath oil she entered the fragrant water. Closing her eyes, she tried to empty her mind.

A quick rattle on the door disturbed her, just as she'd almost managed to wipe her thoughts clean of all things Nathan.

"Erin? Are you still in the tub?"

"Yes," she called back, "and I'm not com-ing out any time soon. Deal with it."

"OK."

There was silence for a while, then there was scratching at the door. Suspicious, she raised her head from the brim, just as the door opened.

Her anger at his intrusion vanished as soon as he appeared in the doorway, triumphantly holding up the break-in tool—a kitchen knife—and wearing her robe, a frilly pink thing her mother had given her for her birthday. Seeing the emerging smile on her lips, Nathan struck a silly pose, confident in his masculinity even when wearing such an exaggeratedly feminine piece of clothing. It was impossible to hold back her guffaws, at least until he threw off the robe and stood there naked, hands on hips, staring down at her, or rather at the bubbles covering her. Her laughter was abruptly cut off as the smile in his eyes notified her of his intentions. She glanced at the frothing water.

"Um, Nathan, if you're thinking about coming in, there really isn't room…"

"I think there is," he replied. "It was the first thing I checked for when you showed me your bathroom." Water sloshed onto the floor as he proceeded to prove it to her. His legs moved deliciously against hers as he slid in opposite her and took her ankles into his hands under the water. "See? Plenty of room."

"Fine. But *you* mop the floor," she muttered, but couldn't sulk any more. He was massaging her calves and she couldn't object to his presence when he was making her feel this good. Slowly, barely an inch at a time, his hands moved up her legs, massaging in leisurely, tortuous circles, and when he had reached her knees the heat was unbearable, although logically she knew the bath-water must have cooled rather than warmed while his hands made their slow journey up her legs.

His fingers made her gasp aloud and strain closer to his hands, but he deprived her of anything more than fleeting contact, the wicked rapture of his touch just out of reach.

She whimpered, and tried to move against his hands, but he just kept up the torment. Frustrated, she reached below the water and grabbed his hands, showing him exactly what she wanted from him.

Nathan laughed in surprised pleasure at her aggressiveness and gave in. He shuddered as she held his wrists, still in control, then grinned, pleased with his lover.

"Let it be my baby, Erin," he groaned. Hell, seducing her into agreeing had worked once, it might work again. Then all he had to do was stop her from retracting it.

"No." Her face was flushed, her utterance strangled, but it was nevertheless a no. He reclaimed his hands and doubled his efforts, then stopped. Her dazed eyes opened, revealed everything to him, showing him the look he was familiar with, even after just one night together. He kept absolutely still, watching the desire in her eyes mingle with confusion.

"Nathan?" she questioned weakly.

"Why not? I'd make a good father. Children need a father. You'd have your baby, and a father who'd be there for him or her. And for you, if you wanted to. We've been doing great together so far. Why not give it a try and see how things go?"

She took a deep breath, the rigid tips of her breasts tempting him as they rose above the water. "Do we have to talk about this now?"

"Yes."

She closed her eyes in frustration. "OK. Because neither of us wants a relationship, remember? I don't want a father for my child."

Not to his displeasure, he noticed there was no mention of a lack of love in her list of whacko reasons. And after last night, he was sure now of his own feelings. Not "might be" any more. He loved her. He wanted a future with her and their child, but her reluctance kept him from revealing his love. He didn't want to put her in a position of having to deny or confess her love for him—because the thought of her not loving him was even scarier than the thought of her returning his feelings. He'd already lost his heart—he didn't want to lose his dignity and pride as well, if it turned out she did not love him. He wouldn't want her pity. Never that. He moved his hands down her legs to her feet, and resumed his massage.

"No father at all, not even a name or a face—that's better than choosing me?"

"Nathan...I don't think you're even thinking clearly. You don't want me and a baby messing up your nomadic life. How can you even be there for the kid when you're on the other side of the world most of the time?"

"I'm thinking about settling down, remember? And I do want you. And you want me." He rubbed at his neck with his free hand. "I've got a hickey to prove it."

Erin blushed and peered at his neck, but he was pleased to see her bite her lip to hide a grin as well. "Nonsense. Only teenagers make hickeys. It's just faintly red. It'll be gone tomorrow."

"Have my baby," he repeated and slid his hands over her again, just to remind her how that conception would happen.

Her eyes closed and her breath caught, but she still shook her head.

"No?" Reluctantly he let her go and leaned back in the tub. "Sorry, Librarian, no baby, no sex."

Her eyes went wide open, radiating frustration and shock and then she was sitting up and glaring at him. *"What?"*

He put his hand on his heart and tried to ignore the outraged and indignant protests of his own body at this ridiculous suggestion. "From now on, you need a specific goal before I'll allow you to seduce me. Either making a baby, or practising for making a baby. No more recreational sex."

"You can't be serious."

"I'm very serious."

She stared at him and he watched her expression slowly fade from outrage into cunning. Then her hands were on his chest, her mouth on his neck and she was whispering into his ear, telling him exactly what he was missing.

"Erin..."

"Yes?"

"You're killing me. But I'm not giving in."

"Fine." She grabbed the sides of the tub and stood up, providing him with an exquisite view before it all got covered up with a towel. "You're leaving in just a few days, aren't you? Imagine all the things we could have done in that time. Your loss." A sound from the bedroom interrupted. "That's your cellphone, isn't it?"

Nathan nodded. "It is. Hand me a towel, will you?"

"Glad to escape, are you?" she muttered, looking so grumpy that he just had to place a kiss on her nose as he grabbed the towel and shot past her to get to his phone.

Nathan noticed Erin move around the room, dry her hair and get dressed, but the phone call took most of his attention. He spoke in low, urgent tones, trying to pick words that wouldn't tell Erin what was going on and give him the chance to explain to her himself, but by her increasingly strained movements he could see he wasn't successful. When he finally could hang up, she had already withdrawn from him.

"Erin..." he began.

CHAPTER EIGHT

"You're leaving," she stated flatly. She wasn't really surprised, but she was shocked at how bereft she felt, being cheated of the few days she'd counted on them having. Only one night, and it was over.

Nathan nodded. "Yes. I have to. Just for a while. It's a fragile political situation in South America, which might turn into a civil war or a revolution. I can't turn this down. But I'll be back soon. I promise."

Erin nodded mutely. Of course he was leaving. And he'd no doubt be back sooner or later. But not back to her. She'd known what she was getting into, spending the night with him. She might love him, but even though he wanted her to have his baby, he didn't want commitment any more than she did. This was fine. This was how it was supposed to be. That sick feeling would pass soon. If she told herself this often enough, she'd eventually start believing it.

Nathan sighed. "I know what you're thinking, Erin. Stop it."

"You have no idea what I'm thinking."

"Yes. You think I'm not coming back."

"It doesn't matter," she shot back, shoving the pain behind a wall of ice. "I already told you. I hope you come back, for Sally's sake, but you don't owe me anything. I just wanted a few days with you. It doesn't change anything about what I want in my life." She bit her lip. "I won't deny I would have liked to have a few days with you, but I'll be fine. It's over now. So come back for Sally, not for me."

He shook his head. "It's not over, Erin. I'll be gone for a little while, then I'm back and we're talking things over."

"Will you be in danger?"

"No more than usual."

She gave a dry laugh. "How reassuring."

"I'll probably be back in less than three weeks, Erin."

"Nathan, I meant what I said. I just wanted a few days, nothing more. I just wanted to get this out of our systems. And I'm glad we had last night. It's fine. I'll be fine."

"Would you please think about us while I'm away? About allowing me to father your child? I want us to make your baby together. You and me. Not you and some nameless, faceless stranger."

She tried to swallow the lump in her throat. "That's not what I want, Nathan. If there was anyone I wanted to father my baby, it would be you, but it would never work out. You're the way you are, and I'm the way I am. Neither one of us has ever wanted a family because we're just not family material. We'd fail miserably, and our child would suffer."

Nathan cursed. "There isn't time to discuss this now, I have to go. We'll postpone this until I get back, OK?"

"There is nothing to postpone."

He grabbed her shoulders and gently shook her. "Don't do this to me now, Erin. Please. I have to go. People are already waiting for me at the airport. Just promise me we'll talk again when I get back."

Miserable, she nodded. There was no choice.

He wrapped one of her curls around his finger and tickled her cheek with the fine hair. "Are you worried about me?"

"Of course we'll worry about you."

Nathan kept stroking her cheek with the curl of her hair. He could almost see her withdrawing from him, climbing into her shell to prevent the hurt. All his life he'd been doing the same thing, and he knew how it felt, and how necessary it was at the same time. He hated leaving her like this, but people were counting on him, waiting for him. "I will be fine. I've been there before and I know the area. I'll be travelling with a reporter friend of mine; we're used to working together. We'll be careful. And I will be back in only three weeks at the most."

Erin nodded, still staring at his chest.

"I'll call you if I can. I don't know how well my cellphone will work over there, but I'll call whenever I can. And you have my number."

Another of those stiff nods. Nathan grabbed his clothes and got dressed, then put his camera away in its bag. There was no more time. He had to leave, but he hated to leave Erin like this. She was just standing there, hugging herself, waiting for him to go away. She looked so alone it broke his heart. Cursing, he put his arms around her, but she did not return his hug.

"Please look at me, Erin."

Her eyes were moist with unshed tears although she bravely tried for a carefree smile. He muttered a curse. The timing was bad. He would have needed a few more weeks to convince her that things could work between them, that it was worth giving a chance. Maybe even get to the stage of risking his heart, telling her how he felt. If all went well, perhaps they could both find the courage to commit to each other despite everything.

"I'm OK, Nathan. I'll be fine. Now, go."

"Sweetheart…"

"Go!" She lifted the camera bag and put it on his shoulder, then turned him around and pushed him towards the front door. "Goodbye, Nathan. Be careful."

Unable to watch him leave, she turned around, shutting the door behind her. Only it didn't shut. Irritated, she turned around to kick whatever it was out of the way, but all of a sudden she was swept off her feet.

Nathan carried her to the couch and sat down with her in his lap. "I…am… coming…back." Each word was punctuated

with a kiss. "Like it or not, I'm coming back
And we are going to make a baby. If you want
a baby, it will be our baby. Yours and mine
Nobody else's."

Erin didn't object. She wound her arms
around his neck and kissed him desperately
touching his face and chest as if trying to
memorize every square inch. His response was
just as enthusiastic, but eventually the de-
mands of time broke into their private world.

Silently they stared at each other. Then Erin
stood up and pulled him up with her. She ad-
justed his shirt and smoothed his hair, her hand
lingering for a moment in the warmth from his
body. Her arms went around him inside the
jacket, and she inhaled the familiar leather
scent as she hugged him close.

"Take good care of yourself, Nathan." She
cupped his cheek and kissed him one last time
"And thank you for everything."

He grabbed his camera bag. "I'll miss you
I…" He hesitated. "You mean so much to me
Erin. I'll be back to show you how much." He
threaded his fingers in her hair and pulled her
close for one last, desperate kiss. Then he
turned around and left.

Erin sank back down on the couch and wrapped her arms around herself. Alone again. The way things should be. She hadn't demanded his promise to come back, and she didn't know why he'd given it. Once before a man had left her, promising to come back. Her college boyfriend had not left her for a war-ravaged foreign country, just for a job in a city two hours away. She'd learned her lesson. He hadn't even bothered to let her know they were officially over before there was someone else in his life.

And she'd made her decision clear to Nathan. He was used to being abandoned, to being rejected. His objections were probably his way of defense, of denying that she was rejecting him. Once he thought it over, he wouldn't come back only to risk being rejected once again. It was safer for him not to. And she was grateful that she'd held back her words of love. This part of her life was over. She'd have to look to the future and keep her time with Nathan as a precious memory.

But would it hurt this badly forever?

She bit back the tears and resolutely found her pocket diary. She counted the days. Nineteen days until the appointment at the clinic. In nineteen days she'd conceive her baby, and finally her life would be back on track.

Two weeks later, Erin was sitting at a fast-food restaurant with her twin, still miserable and still determined not to be.

Nathan hadn't called, but he had got a message across, that he would be out of contact for a while. The message had gone to Sally, not her, and although that was only logical, Erin couldn't make up her mind if that made her feel better or worse. She'd firmly denied to Sally that they were a couple, and dodged any questions about what had happened at Christmas, but she wasn't sure Sally was buying any of it.

She was feeling terribly alone and the need for someone to confide in was overwhelming.

"Great burgers," Erika said between bites. "The spices they put in the cheese make all the difference."

Erin rolled her eyes. Her sister, despite all her health fads and calorie counting, had a weakness for fast food, and approached the subject with all the enthusiasm and vocabulary of a connoisseur of fine cuisine. "Is the chocolate milk shake a good year?'' she enquired, but the sarcasm was lost on Erika, who merely raised her eyebrows in a question as she gobbled down her French fries.

''You finishing yours?''

Erin pushed her plastic tray over the table. ''All yours.''

Erika dived in and there was silence. Erin stared at her twin, thinking. Then she made up her mind. She would tell Erika. She had to have someone to confide in, maybe even someone to accompany her to the clinic. Her twin could be trusted, and, of all people, she should be able to understand.

''I'm going to have a baby,'' she blurted out.

Erika choked on her milk shake. She coughed, her face turning almost the same shade of red as her hair.

''You're pregnant?'' she squealed, causing several people to glance in their direction. ''You're having Nathan's baby?'' She grabbed Erin's hands and squeezed them. ''I'm so happy for you! There aren't many decent guys around, but I do like Nathan. Are you getting married? When is the baby due? You're not showing under that coat, are you? I didn't notice a thing!''

Erin shook her head throughout her sister's monologue. "It's not Nathan's," she said emphatically. "And keep it down, will you? I don't want the entire town to know."

Erika was gaping. "It's not Nathan's?" She plopped her elbows on the table, rested her chin on her hands and leaned towards Erin. "Let me get this straight: you stay celibate until I'm sure you'll be alone for life, and then all of a sudden you're involved with two men at once? Who's the baby's father? You do *know*, don't you?"

Her voice was lower, but not that much lower. Behind her, two teenage boys were openly staring.

Mortified, Erin snatched her sister's milk shake from her grasp and threw it in the pile of wrappings and leftovers. The plastic chair scraped against the tiles as she stood up, motioning Erika to do the same.

"Not another word until we are in the car," she muttered, walking out. Her sister followed, bombarding her with questions.

"I'm not pregnant yet, Erika," she explained once her sister had finally paused for breath. "I'm going to have an artificial insemination. The baby won't have a father. It will just have me."

"What about Nathan?" her sister asked. "I really thought you were in love with him."

"I am," Erin admitted, barely choking out the words. "I was. I'll get over it. He wants the baby to be his, but I can't do that. It would just be one big mess."

"He wants the baby to be his?"

Erin leaned her head against the side-window and nodded, eyes closed. "Yes. He was quite clear on that. He wanted us to make a baby and 'see how things go'."

"Well, that sounds just wonderful! He loves you, Erin. Even I could see that!"

Erin chuckled and opened one eye to look at her sister. "How come you sound like the romantic all of a sudden?" To her surprise, Erika blushed and looked away.

"We're talking about you now," she stated. "What happened? Did you and Nathan break up?"

"There was nothing to break up," Erin sighed. "Nathan doesn't settle down. He's gone. He left on an assignment. He said he would be back, but he won't. Not for long and certainly not for good. Not for me. Not when I've repeatedly told him I don't want his baby.''

''If he says he'll be back, he will be back.''

Erin almost laughed. ''You've met him, what, once, for a few hours, and you think you know him better than I do?''

''Think about it, Erin. Why would he lie to you?''

Erin shook her head. ''It doesn't matter. I know what I want in life, and Nathan is not a part of it. I just want to have my baby and get on with my life.''

''Erin, are you sure about this? What if Nathan does come back?''

''He's not coming back. How long have we known Sally? Three years? In all that time he has visited once, and that was for a few hours. He's not coming back.''

''But if he does,'' Erika persisted, ''how will he feel if he comes back to you and you are carrying some stranger's baby?'' She started. ''Or might he think that it's his baby?''

''No,'' Erin muttered. ''We used protection and he knows I want a donor baby. A father-less baby...'' She looked at her sister, pleading. "You know how things were with us. I want a calm life, just me and my baby."

Erika shook her head. "Erin...I hate to say this, but you are not making sense. Aren't you letting that jerk you dated in college ruin this for you? Not all men are like that."

Erin stared at her sister, almost speechless. "Who are you and what did you do to my cynic of a sister?"

"I'm serious, Erin. Our parents screwed us up, as parents tend to do, and then you had to pick a total jerk as your first serious boyfriend. But pushing Nathan away like that, when you love him, and it's obvious to any idiot that he loves you, just doesn't make any sense at all. You need to give him a chance."

Erin had had enough of people telling her that she wasn't making sense. "Fine," she snapped at her sister. "Judge me if you want, but I am going through with this. I just hope you won't hold it against the baby how he or she came into being. Nathan has never mentioned commitment, or marriage, or love. None of those things. He just wants me to have his baby rather than some stranger's. For all I know, this could be an offer he'd make to any potential sperm-bank customer."

Her sister opened her mouth, but Erin was too disappointed to allow her to continue.

"Just forget you ever heard about this, Erika. Take me home and just forget I ever mentioned it."

Erika didn't reply. She started the car and drove Erin home in silence. The sisters did not speak until the car had stopped.

"When is the…insemination?" Erika asked, fingers tapping the wheel.

"Friday," Erin answered numbly. Only five days to go. Five days and she would be pregnant.

Hopefully. There was no guarantee of success after all, but she hadn't even contemplated the possibility that she might have to make several attempts.

"Would you like me to come with you?"

Erin dredged up a smile at her twin. "Thanks, Erika. It's nice of you to offer, even if you hate the idea of me doing this."

The pace of drumming on the wheel increased. "I'm not against it in principle. I just think that now that you have a perfectly good candidate for a father, you should consider…"

Erin covered her ears. "Don't go there! It's out of the question!"

Erika waved her hand dismissively. "Fine, fine. It's your life. I'll come with you. What time?"

Even before she opened her eyes to the loud buzz of the alarm clock, her thoughts turned to Nathan. Without him, her baby would be conceived today. It would happen in a cold clinic, instead of in a soft bed with their bodies joined together. Her son or daughter would be created by a stranger's seed, squirted inside her womb.

She suddenly felt sick. Scrambling out of bed, she just made it to the bathroom in time.

She stared at her pale face in the bathroom mirror after throwing up. "It's a bit too soon to have morning sickness," she told her reflection. "But I guess I'd better get used to it."

Pushing the negative thoughts aside, she got dressed, forced down breakfast, then called her sister.

Erika was silent as she picked her up, and her car inched towards the clinic, slower than necessary, even in the morning traffic.

"My appointment is in only ten minutes," Erin complained. She felt cold, even dressed in layers of clothes. The chill was probably born of stress rather than outside temperature. In one hour, she reminded herself, in one hour this will all be over. And, hopefully, a new human being would be growing inside her. "Can't you go a little bit faster?"

Erika muttered something, but did speed up the car.

"You haven't heard from Nathan, have you?" Erika asked, but one glare was enough to silence her, and she took the hint and promptly turned on the radio.

Rachel was again at the reception desk, and smiled broadly at them. "Welcome to the New Life Clinic," she iterated. "How may I help you?"

Once in the familiar waiting room, Erin clutched at her sister's hand with both of hers. Her heart was pounding and Erika looked as worried as she did herself. "I'll be fine," Erin tried to convince them both. "It's not a dangerous procedure or anything."

Erika didn't speak. In fact, she hadn't spoken at all since she had asked about Nathan in the car. Erin wondered whether to push her to say something, but decided she didn't want to hear it. Her sister had made her position clear on this issue, but Erin was grateful that she was willing to provide support anyway. She needed someone close by.

Removing her hands from Erika's, she closed her eyes and took a deep breath, then with determination turned to the table for something to read, only to grab the same brochure that had got her in so much trouble last time. The new-found calmness vanished, and after a few minutes it was replaced by intense terror as a young man entered the waiting room, nodded politely at them and sat down opposite them. Erin couldn't help but stare. Could that be the father of her baby? He could have matched the physical description of two of her donors.

She was only slightly relieved when a few minutes later a young blond woman came in and sat by his side, threading her hand with his. Not a donor. Not the father of her baby.

All too soon, and yet not a moment too soon, her name was called. She stood up and started towards the door, but Erika didn't let go of her hand. She looked back at her sister. "What?"

"Erin...are you sure about this?" Erika stood up and pulled Erin with her to a corner. "Don't you think you should wait a while?"

Erin's nerves really couldn't take much more. She yanked her hand out of Erika's grasp and stepped back. "Wait for what? Mr Right to appear? There isn't one, Erika! Of all people, you should know that."

"I'm getting married."

Erin stared at her sister, absolutely certain she must have misheard. "You are what?"

Erika looked out of the window. "To Richard. He proposed last night. I said yes. We're in love. We're getting married." She looked back at Erin. "He's my Mr Right. He did exist after all. And I think Nathan is yours. You shouldn't do this. Even if he hasn't proposed marriage, you should wait for him before doing something like this. You have no idea why he hasn't mentioned commitment as well as having a baby. For one thing, he might not want to mention marriage because he knows how set you are against it. Offering to father your baby might be his way of committing to you. And that's a huge commitment to make, Erin. Especially for someone like Nathan."

"Miss Avery?" Rachel was waiting in the doorway. In a daze, Erin followed Rachel down a hallway and into an examining room, where Dr Roser was waiting. After a short briefing lecture, which she didn't really hear, she was guided behind a curtain to change.

Behind the curtain, Erin took a few deep breaths, grateful for the reprieve. She had to work hard at keeping the news of Erika's engagement out of her mind, or her sister's, the ultimate cynic's, new conviction that love and marriage were indeed possible. The things Erika had said about the possible reasons for Nathan's not mentioning anything about commitment, just the baby, kept up an insistent knocking at the front of her mind, but she was determined to ignore them. She was already here, taking her clothes off in preparation for the operation that would give her a baby. Her mind had been made up a long time ago. There was no use in rethinking things now.

Stress pounded at her temples as she undressed and put on the white gown that the clinic provided. As she hesitantly pushed aside the curtain, she saw a trolley with equipment rolled up towards the examining bench. The stirrups were already in place.

Her eyes were drawn to the equipment cart. Was the sperm she had bought there? The seed that would combine with her own egg to make a child? She covered her mouth with her hand as she felt nauseous again.

The doctor smiled at her, and pointed her towards the bench. Erin walked there, legs trembling, her bare feet sticking to the linoleum. She sat on the bench, then lay down.

Baby, baby, baby, she reiterated, baby, baby, baby. She closed her eyes as her feet touched the stirrups, calling forth a calming image. Her baby. Her baby at her breast, dark hair soft against her skin. Her baby smiling at her from the crib, big green eyes flashing with mirth…

No. No, no, no. This baby would not have green eyes. It could have blue eyes, gray or brown, but it wouldn't have green eyes. None of the donors did.

Suddenly she was no longer lying on the bench, but sitting up, clutching her knees with her arms. ''No!'' she said aloud.

Dr Roser sat down next to her. ''What's wrong, Erin? Cold feet now?''

Erin nodded, tears flowing. Everything seemed very clear now. She wouldn't do this. She couldn't do this, not while loving Nathan. ''I can't go through with it,'' she hiccuped. ''I keep picturing a little dark-haired boy with green eyes.''

The doctor handed her a tissue and patted her arm. ''Good, Erin. This is not something you want to go through with unless you are absolutely certain.''

''I am certain,'' Erin cried. ''I want a baby that's all mine, but the donor doesn't have green eyes.''

Even in the midst of her emotional turmoil she noticed that, as quite a few people had pointed out lately, she wasn't making much sense.

Dr Roser kept up the supply of the much-needed tissues. ''I think this problem won't go away even if we find you a green-eyed donor,'' she commented. ''You have a specific man in mind, don't you?''

Miserably, Erin nodded.

''Is he unable to father children?''

''No. He offered,'' she sniffed.

''What is the problem, then?''

Before she could formulate the answer the door was flung open, and a very angry man strode in, followed by a rather timid-looking Rachel. Erin did a double take. A very angry *bearded* man.

"I told him she'd be out if he only waited a few minutes," Rachel squeaked, "but he wouldn't listen."

Torn between immense relief and utter panic, Erin covered her face in her hands.

"I can't believe you would do this behind my back, Erin!" he all but growled, glaring down at her, before sweeping her off the bench and hugging her so tightly it almost hurt. It did hurt. But it didn't matter. She was in his arms again. She clung to his neck, but didn't dare look at his face. It was too scary. Everything was very scary, but still hope was determined to bloom. Could things work out after all?

The doctor looked at him, then back at her. "I assume this is Mr Green Eyes, Erin?"

She nodded, peeking back at the doctor, but still avoiding Nathan's gaze. Dr Roser closed the door and motioned for the irate Nathan to sit down. Her voice was calming and authoritative and to Erin's relief he obeyed, first putting her down into another chair. He still looked angry when he cupped her face in his hands and forced her to look at him, and she shut her eyes tightly. A cowardly move, but a necessary one at the moment. She was being brave on the inside, allowing all sorts of hopes and dreams to be born—she'd allow herself to be cowardly on the outside.

At least while he looked so darn angry.

"Erin, why didn't you wait for me? I told you I'd be back. We never got a chance to talk things through. Why couldn't you wait? Hell, if I'd known you were still considering this, I never would have left you. It didn't even cross my mind that you'd do this while I was gone."

Erin shivered. He was right. Why hadn't she waited? Why hadn't she trusted him, just enough to wait a few weeks?

"Erin, look at me."

She couldn't. She was trembling too badly.

Nathan cupped her face in his hands and kissed her. "Don't be scared, Erin. We'll work it out. If the insemination worked, I'll love this baby as my own. I won't lie to you—of course I would prefer that it was mine biologically as well, but I'll get over that soon. This baby will never be treated any differently from our other children. I promise. I wouldn't let that happen."

"But…"

"No buts. We're not even talking about this. If there is a baby already, it'll be my baby because it is your baby. Got it? Then we'll see about making some more. You wanted two or three, right? And we're getting married. It's worth the risk, because we'll just make such a terrific family. And don't even think about refusing. If it's what it takes, I'll seduce you right there at the altar until you say yes."

"Nathan…" The tears had started flowing again, but she was also laughing, so she finally opened her eyes. She cupped his cheek in her hand. "I do love you, you know. Even when you're bearded and bossy."

He didn't blink, but stared at her, his eyes worried, and when he finally breathed out she realized he'd been holding his breath. "Do you?"

She nodded. "I do. I have forever. I think our snow fight did it. It's as if I had blinkers on, I was so determined to have things the way I had decided, to avoid making my parents' mistakes and that mistake I'd made once before, trusting a man who wasn't trustworthy. I thought that proved it, that relationships weren't something I could handle. I never expected to fall in love with you."

"I didn't dare hope you loved me," he said quietly. "I didn't even think in those terms. If you'd ask my sister, she'd be only too happy to provide you with her amateur-psychology theories about me having some deep-rooted complex about being unlovable. Perhaps that's it. I don't know. I just wanted to keep you with me any way I could, but I never dared hope you would love me. I wanted to make you like me, want me, need me, and I thought I had succeeded at least at that." He cursed. "I shouldn't have gone away without talking things through. I didn't dare suggest commitment, marriage, or even living together because I knew you didn't want any of that. You just wanted a baby, and I wanted to be the one to give that to you at least. Maybe something more would develop from there." He kissed her forehead and groaned, closing his eyes. "When I heard you were going through with this, I thought I'd lost you. And I regretted so badly that I had never told you that I loved you."

"Well…?" she asked in a tremulous voice, when he didn't continue.

"Well what?"

"Aren't you going to tell me, then?"

Nathan opened his mouth to speak, but was distracted by a soft sigh behind them. Rachel was wiping her eyes with a gauze while the doctor was grinning from ear to ear.

"It seems like you have your own personal donor right here, Erin," Dr Roser said, pushing a somewhat reluctant Rachel out of the door. "I think we'll give the two of you some privacy now. Take all the time you need. You know the way out. And do come again, should you ever require our services." She smiled, and left, shutting the door behind her.

Erin could hardly see her own personal donor through the fog of tears, but she heard him chuckle as he turned back to her and put his hand on her stomach. "I think we should be married as soon as possible. I'd like us to be settled in by the time the baby comes."

"Nathan...there is no baby."

His gaze snapped up to hers. "What?"

She gestured towards the door. "That's why she said you were my personal donor. I couldn't go through with it. I kept imagining your baby, the baby you offered to give me. And I just couldn't. I wanted your baby."

Nathan lifted her onto his lap and hugged her quietly for a while. "I won't lie to you, Erin, and tell you I'm not overjoyed. I am."

"I'm afraid, Nathan."

"I know. So am I. But we're adults, Erin. We are not kids who get in too deep too soon. You are not your mother and I am not your father. Life is about taking risks. And love is about trust. We'll be fine. I promise."

"You forgot to say you loved me, Nathan."

He cleared his throat. "I love you." He wrapped his arms around her and squeezed so tightly she could hardly breathe. "I love you, love you, love you."

Erin giggled. "That wasn't so hard, was it?"

"No." He laughed, and kissed her hard. His beard stung her face, but she didn't mind. "In fact, it feels so good I might be telling you every two minutes from now on."

Erin wiped away her tears with the back of her hand. "I forgot. Erika…she's in the waiting room; I should let her know I'm OK…"

"She's gone home," Nathan said.

Erin's head snapped up. How Nathan had come to be here hadn't crossed her mind yet. "She told you I was here?" she asked, outraged. "That's why you knew where to find me? How dare she interfere…?"

Nathan covered her mouth with his hand. "Before you get out the tar and feathers, think it over."

Erin did. Somewhat mollified, she snuggled closer into Nathan's arms. "You're right," she muttered. "She knows me better than I know myself. She probably knew I wouldn't go through with it."

Above her head, she felt Nathan shake his head. "She was sure you would go through with it. It wasn't easy to get hold of me, you know. A whole army of people was involved in getting the message to me and a bigger one to get me out of there so quickly. She said I had to get here before it was too late, that there was nothing she could do to change your mind. When I met her out in the waiting room, she was about to come in here herself and cause trouble."

"Erika is turning into a romantic." Erin smiled. "I hope everything works out for her and Richard. I like him." She reached to his face, stroking his beard. "You look tired."

He chuckled. "I've been travelling non-stop for almost thirty hours." His face changed and he looked intently into her eyes. "You know, Erin, that if I had been too late and you were already pregnant I would have loved that child as my own?'' His eyes searched her face. ''I was afraid that you would think I wouldn't love that child. I would.''

She cupped his cheek in her hand. ''Sally told me about your parents. How they treated you after she was born.''

The shutters came down in his eyes, but only for a second before he pushed them away and allowed her a glimpse inside. ''She had no business telling you that.''

''I think she knows I love you. I've been denying it until I'm blue in the face, but she keeps bringing up your name and giving me sly looks.'' She put her arms around him. ''It was so cruel the way they treated you. Most parents love their adoptive children just as much as their biological ones. I can't understand them.''

''My parents were good people, Erin. Don't blame them. They couldn't help themselves. It was never deliberate on their part. I understood. After all, Sally was their flesh and blood, I was a distrustful and scared five-year-old who insisted on locking my bedroom door for two years after I got there. And anyway, by then I had already seen the back of my biological folks and a few sets of foster parents. I could take it.''

The complete lack of either anger or self-pity in his voice moved her. ''Aren't you angry?''

''Yes, I'm angry,'' he said in a flat tone of voice that belied the words. ''But I have no right to be. They may not have been the perfect parents, but without them I would have been raised in an orphanage or a succession of foster homes. I owe them for many things, but I don't owe them my anger any more than they owed me their love.'' He shook his head when she opened her mouth to protest. ''That's just how it is, Erin. Let it be.''

She had to ask. ''What about Sally? Didn't you...? Why did you stay away from Sally?''

He took her hand in his and gently kissed her palm. ''I went to see my biological parents once, a long time ago. They were...less than pleased. At that time, my feelings about just about everything seemed to freeze up, and I went away to Europe with nothing more than the expensive camera that my parents had given me for my eighteenth birthday.'' He took a deep breath. ''It was such a relief to be away. I threw myself into my work, and I was lucky to be in the right place at the right time. I almost got killed, but I also sold my first pictures and made my name relatively quickly. And after that I just kept going. I told myself that it was better for everyone involved if I just stayed away. My work was very dangerous, and they would only worry more if they knew.''

He clasped her hands between his and stared down for a while before continuing. ''I came home for my mother's funeral. My father was very upset that I hadn't come home to see her while she was sick. He disregarded the fact that she had refused to allow them to tell me how serious it was. Anyway, he was beside himself with grief, and he told me that if it had been up to him he'd never have taken in the filthy orphan I'd been.'' He took a deep breath. ''I stayed for the funeral, and then I just left. I allowed my anger to control me and left. And when he died, only a year later, it was easier to stay away. I told myself it was too late. And I took the easy way out. It's not a good excuse, Erin; I was a bastard to do that to my sister. I'll just have to hope I can make it up to her now that I'm settling down close by.''

His voice was hard. Erin removed one of her hands from his grasp and ran it through his hair, comforting him. He squeezed her hand so tightly it almost hurt and his head tilted forward until she couldn't see his face any more. "Again, if you'd ask Sally to dig into my psyche, she'd probably say that I was afraid you couldn't love me, any more than other people could. And she might tell you too that I was afraid I wasn't really capable of love."

Erin smiled tenderly at his clumsy, roundabout way of expressing those difficult feelings. "I know," she murmured. Some day he would share more of his painful story with her and she could help him heal, as he would her. Enough tears had been shed today. It was time to smile, to laugh.

To play.

She looked at Nathan, then glanced speculatively around. "Nathan, have you ever been in a sperm bank before?"

He shook his head, his expression one of relief at the end of their serious conversation. "No. I'm afraid I don't have dozens of my biological offspring running around out there."

Erin smiled. "Good. I want a monopoly on your genes." She unzipped his leather jacket and pushed it off his shoulders. Her fingers ran gently over his chest. "Would you like to make a donation?"

The shocked expression on his face was priceless. "*What?*"

"There is a lock on the door," she whispered as she opened the buttons of his black shirt one by one, exposing his chest to her hands and mouth. "And there is this examining bench, just waiting for a willing donor."

Nathan glanced around to where she pointed, then down at her hands and then back up at her face. "What? You don't mean... You can't mean... No... Here...? You're joking, aren't you?"

She opened her gown and pulled him close, revelling in feeling his hard chest against her breasts, almost as much as she reveled in the shock in his face. She rested her head on his shoulder, her mouth close to his ear. "I came here for a purpose, Nathan. Let's make that baby."

After several tense seconds his hand cupped her cheek and turned her face to his. He kissed her lightly, then moved a few inches away. "Uh-uh."

"Uh-uh? What do you mean, uh-uh?"

"Remember what I told you last time? No baby, no sex? I've changed my mind. Now it's no marriage, no sex."

She stared up into his teasing green eyes. All shadows had been chased off, and she felt she was really seeing him for the first time, seeing directly into his soul, filled with love for her.

"No sex before we're married?" Her hands moved over him, strategically skimming over all his sensitive places.

"Right. First I'm getting you to a church, and a ring on your finger, not to mention a bed that's bigger than your small one. No sex until then."

"I see. No sex. How about a sperm donation?"

"What?" He grabbed her wrists as she began pulling at his clothes again. "You're not undressing me. This is not happening."

Unperturbed, she made her way onto his lap and started nuzzling his neck. "Doesn't it sound intriguing, though?" She pulled her wrists free and slid her hands inside his clothes wherever she could make a gap. ''Are you absolutely sure, Nathan? No sex? Not even a simple donation?''

''I suppose...it wouldn't really be sex...'' he conceded.

''Exactly. It would just be a donation.'' She kissed him and felt his body tremble as he fought a losing battle with himself.

''I can't believe this. Damn it, Erin... We can't... This is crazy, you know—Erin!''

MILLS & BOON® PUBLISH EIGHT LARGE PRINT TITLES A MONTH. THESE ARE THE EIGHT TITLES FOR SEPTEMBER 2003

❧

THE BILLIONAIRE BRIDEGROOM
Emma Darcy

THE SHEIKH'S VIRGIN BRIDE
Penny Jordan

AN ENIGMATIC MAN
Carole Mortimer

AT THE PLAYBOY'S PLEASURE
Kim Lawrence

THE INDEPENDENT BRIDE
Sophie Weston

THE ORDINARY PRINCESS
Liz Fielding

FIANCÉ WANTED FAST!
Jessica Hart

BABY CHASE
Hannah Bernard

MILLS & BOON®

Live the emotion